Kinsale Kisses

By Elizabeth Maddrey

Scripture quoted by permission. Quotations designated (NIV) are from THE HOLY BIBLE: NEW INTERNATIONAL VERSION®. NIV®. Copyright © 1973, 1978, 1984 by Biblica. All rights reserved worldwide.

Cover design by HopeSprings Books.
Cover art photos ©iStockphoto.com/vladans and ©iStockphoto.com/risamay, used by permission.

Published in the United States of America by Elizabeth Maddrey
www.ElizabethMaddrey.com

Publisher's Note: This novel is a work of fiction. Names, characters, places, and incidents are either products of the author's imagination or used fictitiously. All characters are fictional, and any similarity to people living or dead is purely coincidental

ISBN-13: 978-0692310922

Other Books by Elizabeth Maddrey

A is for Airstrip: A Missionary's Jungle Adventure

The 'Grant Us Grace' Series
Book One: Wisdom to Know
Book Two: Courage to Change
Book Three: Serenity to Accept

Novellas in the 'Grant Us Grace' world
Joint Venture

Novels in the 'Grant Us Grace' world
The 'Remnants' Series:
Book One: Faith Departed
Book Two: Hope Deferred
Book Three: Love Defined

For my sister.

Thank you for believing in me.

Rachel Sullivan hitched up her backpack, tugging the shoulder strap tighter to fix it in place and dragged her suitcase through the automatic doors of Ireland's Shannon Airport. Maybe she should have taken her Aunt Siobhan's advice and flown into the Cork airport. But flying direct was simpler than dealing with changing planes in Amsterdam, London, or Paris. She glanced at the tag dangling from the key in her hand. Her rental car was in spot E37. Large lettered signs identified rows, and Rachel angled toward the bright green E half-way across the lot. As she crossed the pavement, she read the white numbers painted at the end of the parking spaces. Thirty-five. Thirty-six. She stopped in front of a tiny silver car, her jaw falling open. She'd said compact but this was…miniscule. At five-foot-nine, Rachel wasn't huge, but she doubted there'd be more than two feet left over if she were to stretch out on the ground with her head at the front bumper.

Reaching over the top of the roof she could touch the seam of the passenger door.

Shaking her head, she pushed the trunk release on the key fob. It looked like there was room for her luggage, though it was good she'd packed light. She heaved her suitcase up and wiggled it into the space between the wheel well bumps. After pushing the hatchback down, she pulled open the door, tossed her backpack to the other side, and sat.

"Wrong side." Muttering, she stood and cast a furtive glance around the lot. No one seemed to have noticed her. That was something at least. She circled the car, moved her backpack from the driver's seat, and settled behind the steering wheel. Everything looked straightforward. At least the turn signal and windshield wipers weren't backward too. But...her gaze landed on the gear shift. A manual. Great. Dad had insisted she learn to drive a manual in high school. A pang shot through her heart as images of their driving lessons flitted through her memory. She'd switched to an automatic when she bought her first car and hadn't looked back. Was it too much to hope it was like riding a bike?

She studied the shifter and took a deep breath, pressed down the brake and the clutch, and turned the key. The engine purred like an anemic cat. She wasn't going to be doing any racing in this thing, that was for sure. With only the tiniest crunch of the gears, Rachel shifted into reverse and backed out of the parking spot. She wasn't going to think about how she'd rolled down the window the first time she'd tried to shift. Now she just had to make it the rest of the two hour drive to Kinsale on the Southwestern coast in County Cork.

Horns blared at her as she turned right out of the parking lot onto the main road and directly into oncoming traffic. Rachel swerved into the left lane, her heart accelerating past the speed limit as her stomach dropped. Shaking, she gripped the steering wheel. Left. They drive on the left. Glancing in the rearview mirror at the friendly beep behind her, she sped up, unrolling her window when she reached for the gearshift. With the car finally cruising along, she let her gaze roam, ever so slightly, around the countryside.

Rich green was everywhere she looked, though the fields were broken with splotches of black and white. Sheep. Enormous herds of sheep roamed across the emerald land, short gray stone walls separating one herd from another. Squat, one-story cottages nestled at the far end of the fields. Even from a distance the houses looked charming. No thatched roofs, though. At least not that she could see from the road.

There was a bit of traffic as Limerick grew on the horizon. Houses were clumped closer together, looking very much like the suburbs of any small American city, if you could get past the old-world feel that clung to everything. Crossing the Shannon River, she saw signs for the motorway that would take her south. As she took the exit, the suburbs melted back into green fields. Rachel let out a breath. This was the Ireland she'd been expecting. Craving. The fields and sheep offered peace, and that had been in short supply since Dad passed away. Between hospital bills and past-due notices for his business, Rachel had spent the last two months scrambling to find a solution that would let her stay in her childhood home on the Virginia-West Virginia border. But Dad had been using the slim income from their rental cabins to pay down the hospital bills from her mother's ten-year battle with cancer, leaving nothing for repairs and maintenance. And no one wants to rent shabby cabins, no matter how near the ski slopes they are. In the end, she'd had to sell.

The drive through the center of Cork City left Rachel sweating and shaking. Navigating traffic circles was difficult on the best of days, but jetlag added an interesting twist. She'd only gone around the one three times before finding her exit. After that, it was an easy, gentle drive toward the coast. She caught a few glints of sun reflecting off impossibly blue water as she neared Kinsale.

Though the town was a good size, it didn't feel like a city. The increasingly narrow, winding streets cemented the small town image, as did the decent-sized pieces of land surrounding the houses. She rounded a tight corner and came face-to-face with a house she'd recognize anywhere. The mansard roof was out of place among the more traditional peaked roofs. But the jutting stone chimneys, wrought iron balconies, and a bay window across one entire side of the house, facing Kinsale Bay, had been on every Christmas card her aunt had sent for the last twenty-seven years. And probably before then. Sea Haven B&B had been a fixture in their family for two generations. If all went well, Rachel would be the key to ensuring its survival for a third.

She parked next to a sparkling red Mini Cooper. That couldn't possibly be Aunt Siobhan's, could it? Did seventy-something-year-old women drive Minis? It had to be a guest. Leaving her luggage for later, she pocketed the key to her rental and strode to the front door. It was good to be out of the car and moving again. The door sprang open and her petite aunt waved vigorously as she pushed open the screen.

"There you are. I was just beginning to worry." Aunt Siobhan's smile was welcoming.

Tears pricked Rachel's eyes as she wrapped her arms around her aunt's frail shoulders.

"How was the drive then?"

Rachel groaned. "I got the hang of it about two miles—kilometers, I guess—back."

Siobhan chuckled. "I drove in America the one time I came to visit your father. I imagine you feel like I did—everything on the wrong side and the wrong sizes. Your lanes are so huge, you can practically get lost in them."

"Well, at least you don't run the risk of swapping paint with passing cars while still being between the lines." Rachel shook her head. "I'll get used to it, I'm sure."

"Of course you will. Now," Siobhan glanced down at the delicate gold watch on her wrist, "you must be famished. And exhausted. We've no guests at the moment, so I thought we'd walk down to the pub for a bite. Save ourselves the hassle of cleaning up after. But why don't you grab your things and we'll get you settled first."

Rachel returned to the car and dragged her luggage out of the trunk, hefting it up the short flight of stairs to the front door. She followed Aunt Siobhan to the family rooms behind the kitchen, separate from the guest areas.

"Here now. You've your own en suite and a little sitting area as well so we won't be always tripping over one another. Take a few minutes to freshen up and then we'll head on down. It's early yet, so be as long as you like."

Rachel watched her aunt disappear down the hall then turned to take in her room. It was a good-sized space, immaculate and stylishly decorated. The warm, wooden head and footboard matched the nightstands, dresser, and the table and chair across the room. Two camel-backed chairs in a blue damask angled toward one another, sharing a matching footstool. The bed was piled with pillows and a heavenly-looking duvet. If only she could stretch out, just for a moment, and see if it was as comfortable as it seemed. No. After dinner she could rest for as long as she wanted. For now…she'd best do as Aunt Siobhan suggested.

Flipping her suitcase open, she grabbed her bathroom bag from the top and crossed to what had to be the en suite. Gleaming white fixtures from the early 1900s greeted her. She'd never seen antiques in such good shape. She turned the hot water tap and smiled as steam accompanied the liquid pouring out of the faucet.

Rachel spent a few minutes washing her face and reapplying the few dabs of makeup she bothered with. She pulled her chestnut hair into a ponytail and wished, for the millionth time, that it was either the flaming red of her mother or the rich black of her father's family. How, with Irish ancestors on both sides, had she ended up a plain old brunette? It was a mystery some geneticist needed to solve. Maybe they already had, biology hadn't been her strong suit in high school. Even Aunt Siobhan had been a strawberry blonde, before her hair turned white with age.

On her way back through the bedroom, Rachel tugged her wallet from the backpack and slipped its strap over her wrist.

"Ready when you are, Aunt Siobhan."

Rachel threaded her arm through her aunt's as they strolled down the hill toward town. It was only a few blocks, but she'd feel the steepness of the incline on the way back up. As they arrived in Kinsale proper, the houses sat closer together, their bright stucco exteriors forming a kaleidoscope of color. Bed and Breakfast signs hung from the front of many of the buildings that otherwise looked like regular homes.

"You've got a lot of competition, don't you?"

"Ah now, there's plenty of tourism to go around. We do all right, you'll see. It's early yet, the season hasn't properly begun. Here we are, then."

Siobhan stopped in front of a dark green building. Large windows spanned either side of the wooden door and gold letters spelled out the pub's name.

"The Flat Tire?" Rachel raised her eyebrows. "That's not…"

"What, dear? They can't all be called O'Malley's, you know. Come along."

Her aunt opened the door and a wild flurry of violin music poured into the street. Rachel followed in her aunt's wake.

"There's herself, then. Come to see me at last, have ya?" A man who had to be in his seventies winked at Siobhan. "And who is it you've brought?"

"Now, Patrick McTeague, get on with you. This is my niece Rachel, come from America just today."

Patrick extended his hand across the gleaming wood of the bar, "Pleasure. Though I'm sorry to hear of your father's passing. He and I were mates, back in the day before he left for America and your mother."

Rachel offered a faint smile as she shook his hand. "Thank you."

"Take a seat where you can find one. We've some fine music this evening, for all he's a Yank himself, he knows his way about the fiddle and bodhran well enough and he's a voice that'll make the faeries weep." Patrick nodded, wiping the bar with his rag as he moved to where a customer called to him.

"Why don't you take that booth over by the corner, Rachel? I've a mind to sit a spell with Doreen Nealey. I'll find you in a bit."

"But—" Her aunt's gentle shove set her moving in the direction of an empty booth before she could get out another word. She turned and watched as her aunt and Doreen greeted one another with a long hug. Then both women pulled knitting from their purses and began to work, their mouths moving a mile a minute. *All right. I'm a big girl. It's not the first time I've eaten in a restaurant alone.*

Rachel wove through the tables in the dim pub. There was scarcely enough light to see, but the creamy hue of the bulbs added to the ambiance. She could easily imagine losing track of time in a place like this. The music stopped as she slid onto the hard bench. A smattering of applause greeted the end of the tune.

"Thank you."

Rachel's gaze snapped to the owner of the rich baritone voice. His dark brown hair was fashionably spiked on top and neatly trimmed. Steel blue eyes looked out beneath long lashes. A hint of stubble grew on a full, square jaw and a smile tugged at the corners of his lips, as if he was enjoying a joke that no one else knew. Her stomach fluttered. Of course, she knew the men in Ireland were supposed to be handsome. That was the only reason her best friend had agreed that this trip was a good idea. It seemed married people were determined to see all their friends married off, too. Rachel wasn't opposed to the idea, but the pool of eligible men at home seemed particularly shallow.

The man looped a guitar over his shoulder and began picking the opening strains to a familiar tune. What was the song's name. When his rich, full voice added the lyrics, her heart stopped. Surely he was a professional musician with a major recording contract, not simply a pub singer? But no, the barkeep, Patrick, had said he was an American?

A waitress dressed in all black and toting a tray of empty pint glasses paused at her booth. "I'll be right with you. Did ya' want something from the bar?"

"Um, no. A Coke?"

"Sure. Were you eating tonight, too?"

Rachel's stomach rumbled. When had she eaten last? The day was a blur—even the trauma of driving from the airport was beginning to fade. "I'd like to…is there a menu?"

The waitress nodded to a tall, laminated card stuck behind the salt and pepper shakers against the wall of the booth. "I'll get your Coke while you look that over. You're American, yeah?"

Rachel's eyebrows shot up but she nodded.

"I'll add ice then for you, yeah?" The woman sauntered off before Rachel could answer. Maybe it hadn't been a question.

Four Green Fields. The name of the song popped into her head and she pursed her lips. Such a sad song, filled with the bitterness of Ireland's history. And yet…a tinge of hope at the end. Her father always told her the Irish were champions of embracing their pain but still finding something to celebrate. You just had to listen to their music to see it. If only her dad could see her here, in his hometown, at a booth in a pub listening to traditional music. He would've been delighted. He'd always planned to bring her and Mom to Ireland. Then Mom got sick and Rachel…well, she hadn't reacted well. Regret washed through her.

Pushing those thoughts aside, she plucked the menu from its spot by the wall and scanned the offerings. The waitress reappeared and slid a soda in front of her as the music ended.

"What can I get you?"

"A bowl of the potato soup, please."

With a nod, the waitress sashayed away, stopping at each of her tables as she wound her way back to the bar.

The musician set his guitar aside before he hopped down from the raised platform wedged in the corner of the room and strode after the server. He tapped her on the shoulder and, after a brief conversation, nodded in Rachel's direction. The server smiled and disappeared behind a swinging door.

The man paced back across the pub and paused by Rachel's table, offering an impish smile, a dimple forming in his right cheek. "Hi there. Can I join you? It's a bit crowded now and I'm due for a break."

Rachel cleared her throat and glanced around. It had filled up. "Um. Sure." She gestured to the space across from her. "Have a seat. I'm Rachel."

His smile broadened and he lowered himself to the bench. "Colin O'Bryan. It's a pleasure to meet you. Have you been in Ireland long?"

She shook her head. "Just arrived today. I'm visiting my aunt for a bit. What about you?"

"I landed in Dublin about a month ago, but got to Kinsale just yesterday. I've been making my way from town to town, singing for my supper and a place to lay my head."

Rachel blinked. "You mean you've booked a tour, right? Have dates and locations lined up where they're expecting you? Obviously you do this for a living back home as well."

His deep laugh rose above the hum of conversation in the room. "Oh no. This is just a hobby in the States. But most towns have a pub or two looking for a musician for one evening or, if you're lucky, a few in a row. And now I've a few references as well that help pave the way. If I can't find a spot, then I find a room for the night and still get to see whatever sights there are to be had."

The server appeared with two steaming bowls of soup and a plate piled with thick slices of brown bread. She set them down, added a dish of butter and a small teapot, and scooted away before Rachel could murmur her thanks.

"Mind if I say grace?"

Rachel pulled her attention back to Colin. He wanted to pray? With a complete stranger? "No. Of course not."

She bowed her head then glanced up hastily as his fingers closed around hers. His touch sent tingles flying up her arm.

"Heavenly Father, thank you for bringing Rachel safely to Ireland today and for providing me with a place to sing and rest this evening. Bless this food and the hands that prepared it. Amen."

"Amen." Rachel gave her hand a little tug, unwinding her fingers from his. She stirred her soup, inhaling the earthy aroma as it spiraled up from the bowl. "For how long?"

Colin broke a piece off a slice of bread and dunked it in his soup. "How long what?"

"How long will you do the traveling musician thing? If you've been here a month, you must be nearing the end of your vacation time."

He grinned and dunked another chunk of bread. "Let's just say I'm currently unencumbered with trivial details like vacation and sick days."

"Ah." Great. He was unemployed. She was too, but at least she wasn't content with the situation. She was working on a solution. He was wandering around a foreign country like a nineteen-year-old backpacker with no cares in the world. A killer smile and electric tingles only went so far—there were boys at home who could provide those. If she wanted anyone at all, he had to, at least, be a man. It was all moot anyway, she hadn't come here looking for a husband and Colin was probably on the first bus out of town in the morning.

"What about you? How long will you stay?"

Rachel savored the rich flavors of potato, leek, and cream before she swallowed. "Through July. Maybe longer, depending on how things go."

Humor danced in his eyes. "What about your own vacation days?"

Heat flooded her face. She sipped her Coke, grateful for the ice. "How did you put it? I'm currently unencumbered by such things. But I'm looking to see that's not the case for long."

He arched a brow but said nothing.

"Not that it's any of your business, but I just buried my father and sold our family business. My aunt is the only living relative I have and, as you can see, she's in her early seventies." Rachel nodded across the room to where Siobhan knitted with her friend. "Her B&B can barely keep afloat and she's not able to handle the workload anyway. I have a degree in hospitality and grew up in the business. So I'm going to help, and, I hope, make a new home for myself here, in the town my father left as soon as he was of age. So keep your little superior smile to yourself. I may not have a job now, but I'm working on it, not kicking back, singing tra-la-la as if bills don't have to be paid."

Colin scraped the last bite of soup from his bowl and stood. "I'm sorry to hear about your dad. Thanks for letting me share your table."

Mouth agape, Rachel watched as he resumed his place by his instruments. He cast a long look in her direction and then, with a slight smile, picked up his concertina and launched into *The Wild Rover*.

Colin watched Rachel as he sang. Did she know the song? Ah, there it was, a spark of recognition. It didn't actually have a tra-la-la chorus, but it was close enough. What had drawn him to sit with her? Patrick had a staff table in the kitchen, but Colin had wanted to meet the lovely woman sitting by herself and the full pub had provided the perfect excuse. Too bad she was a bit of a snob.

He'd dated worse. Much worse, in fact. But that was part of the reason he was here singing for his supper. Jessica had seen to it that there was nothing left for him in Chicago. Selling his half of the business had given him enough of a nest egg that he was free to do as he chose for as long as he liked. With his grandmother's stories of Ireland whispering in his ear, he'd booked the first flight he could find. He hadn't questioned the decision since and wasn't going to start simply because a stranger disapproved of his choices without understanding the reasons behind them.

Putting aside the small accordion, he picked up his fiddle and dove into a cheery jig. Colin smiled when he saw Rachel's foot begin to tap. He forced his attention away from her, his gaze skimming over the tables filled with families and clusters of friends. Men sat at the bar watching the TV and slapping one another on the back depending on how the soccer—football, they called it football here—game was progressing. It was a homey, friendly feeling, and not one unique to this pub. He hadn't been anywhere in Ireland yet where he hadn't found it. Good craic, as the locals would say. Even in the bigger cities, there was community.

He frowned slightly as Rachel stood and crossed to a table where two older women sat knitting. She pressed a kiss to the cheek of the smaller, elf-like woman. That must be her aunt, though if there was a family resemblance, it wasn't obvious from here. Despite her attitude, something about Rachel was compelling. Who was she, really? And why did the mere thought of her fingers curved around his for something as simple as a meal-time prayer leave him short of breath?

When the last customer shuffled out the door, singing loudly on the arm of his friend, Colin hopped down from the platform.

"Toss me a rag, I'll help wipe down tables."

"You sure? It's not part of your deal." Patrick ducked behind the bar, popping back up with a spray bottle and white cloth.

"Sure. It's the least I can do. Your customers are good tippers." Colin grinned and squirted a table before beginning to scrub vigorously.

"Only when the music is fine. You're a credit to your blood."

"That's my gran's doing." Colin scoured the chairs then flipped them up onto the table he'd just cleaned. "She always hoped I'd make it to Ireland. I just wish she'd lived to see it."

"Ah well. She knows, I wager." Patrick stacked glasses in a tub and slid it down the bar where a dishwasher waited to lug it to the kitchen sink. "I saw you met our other Yank, did ya' get along then?"

Colin scoffed. His hand tightened on the cleaning bottle, sending a spray of liquid onto his chin. "I wouldn't say that, no. I don't think she's one who appreciates the company of traveling musicians."

"Hmm. Siobhan seemed to think she was taken with you." Patrick tapped a finger against his lip. "I suppose time will tell."

Colin wasn't going to be around long enough for time to tell, but there was no reason to mention that so he simply continued cleaning. "There's a story with you and Siobhan though, isn't there?"

Patrick leaned on the bar, propping his chin in his hand. "Aye, there is. She's the love of me life and that's for sure."

"Then why aren't you married with great-grandchildren running around your feet? She's clearly just as keen on you."

A wistful smile covered the old man's face. "I always thought there would be. But…twasn't to be."

"But…"

Patrick shook his head and hefted another tub of glasses, backing through the swinging doors.

Colin sighed. Maybe Rachel's snobbery was an inherited streak. He finished the last table and carried his rag into the kitchen. "All set."

"Thanks a million." Patrick looked up from his seat at the staff table. "Will you sing again tomorrow night or do ya' need to be moving on?"

"Can I let you know in the morning?"

"Of course. Go on up now, and have a good rest. Your instruments are fine out in the pub 'til morning."

Colin climbed the steep stairs tucked in the back corner of the kitchen to the small apartment above the pub. Patrick had explained that it had been his place, until his mother took ill. She'd passed away earlier in the year and he was living in her house a few blocks away until he figured out what to do. It was simply furnished, all the essentials and very little else. The main room had a hotplate, sink, and mini-fridge tucked in one corner. A sofa and TV sat across from one another with a threadbare woven rug between them. There was a little table next to one end of the sofa. Next to the bathroom was a second, tinier room. The double bed and its brass frame filled the space, with barely enough room for a three-drawer dresser and a tall, skinny wardrobe for a handful of hanging items. A braided rag rug in shades of red brightened the floor.

He toed off his shoes and padded to the bathroom. He'd intended to move on after tonight, but Rachel was an intriguing conundrum. As annoying as he'd found her attitude, he couldn't escape his attraction. Maybe she was worth getting to know better. Would she even let him? He'd stick around a few days and find out.

ELIZABETH MADDREY

4

Rubbing her eyes, Rachel tightened the belt of her robe and shuffled into the kitchen. "Morning."

Siobhan looked up from her Bible. "Good morning. Let me get you some tea. Or do you prefer coffee?"

"Coffee. But I can get it. Don't get up." Rachel poked through the cupboards until she found the ground beans. After a few mistakes, she got the machine brewing and pulled out the chair opposite her aunt. "Did you have a nice time with your friend last night?"

"I did, yes." Siobhan smiled and tucked a bookmark in the pages of her Bible before letting it close. "We often knit together in the evenings. She's working on a bunting for her next grandchild, due this summer."

Rachel tilted her head at the wistfulness in her aunt's voice. "Why did you never marry, Aunt Siobhan?"

"Ah, well. I've only ever loved one man and he…well, I believe he loves me. But he's from a staunch Catholic family and we've been Protestant since the Scots first came to the island."

"I didn't realize that mattered as much anymore." Rachel stood when the coffee maker beeped. She filled a mug and returned to the table.

"Oh, maybe not as much now, but when we were young enough for marriage to make sense it did. Even then, Patrick would have married me, had his mother not put her foot down. He wouldn't cross her while she was living."

"Patrick? From The Flat Tire? That Patrick?" Rachel chuckled. "That explains why it's your favorite pub."

Pink tinged Siobhan's cheeks. "Its menu is good, too. And I can walk there. But yes, Patrick has a lot to do with my visits of an evening. Or at least he did when I started…now it's as much habit as anything."

"But why didn't you marry after his mother died? If that was the only thing stopping you…"

"She passed in January. When I feel uncharitable, I think she held on to the ripe old age of ninety-eight just to spite me." Siobhan offered a sad, thin smile. "Enough about that. As yet we've no bookings for tonight, though that can always change. Until then, why don't you take a look around? Maybe walk out to the fort or down to the bay to see the boats racing?"

"I was going to go through the books and look over the rooms, dive right in."

"No, no." Siobhan waved a hand in front of her face. "We can do that this evening. You should stretch your legs and see a bit of the area."

Rachel studied her aunt. She wanted to see the country, it was true. But she hadn't come here as a tourist. She was supposed to be helping rejuvenate the B&B. How was she going to do that if she didn't get started right away? But she didn't want to start off on the wrong foot with her aunt either. It wasn't as if she'd grown up with Siobhan and knew her well enough to press the issue. At best, they were friendly acquaintances, connected by blood. No matter how much she wanted to take over here, the best course of action was going to be to, as her Dad always used to say, make haste more slowly.

"All right. I'll drive over to the fort and take a look around."

"Don't drive, m'dear. Walk. It's just two kilometers, maybe a tad more, and right along the coast. You'll get some fresh air, stretch your legs, probably even catch sight of a few sailboats."

Rachel glanced down at her feet, still slightly swollen from the airplane. Were they going to hold up? How many miles were in a kilometer? Two? Or was it the other way around? Why had she never paid attention to the metric system? She forced a smile. "Okay, you sold me. I'll go for a walk."

Siobhan nodded. "I'll fix you something to take along while you get ready."

Rachel tightened the shoulder straps of her backpack and took in a deep breath. The tang of salt filled her nostrils. A stone wall separated the road from the rippling water and she watched in fascination as crying gulls swooped over the pebbly beach. At least there wasn't much traffic. She was walking on the yellow line next to the wall with nowhere to go if two cars tried to pass on the single lane that served as a bi-directional roadway here. Sidewalks didn't seem to be a priority either.

Gradually the beach faded into the rocky side of a hill. Her calves burned as she climbed the steep grade. Why hadn't she driven? The views were breathtaking—she would have missed those. But so far, everywhere she'd looked in Ireland had ended with a view so spectacular it didn't seem real. Her aunt had insisted it wasn't going to rain, but she'd tucked her windbreaker into her backpack just in case. For now, it was a pleasant, somewhat sunny morning in late March and the lightweight cornflower blue sweater she'd pulled on with her jeans was almost too warm. The ground leveled out at the top of the hill. Now the other side of the stone wall held a tiny bit of grass before a drop of at least fifty feet to the water.

She had to be nearly there, didn't she?

Finally, the road widened into a parking area and a roped off path angled down terraced patches of bright green grass, all neatly mowed. Even more stone walls rose at the end of the path, meeting in sharp corners before continuing around. She ducked into the visitor's center. The tiny room held t-shirts, stuffed animals, and a small assortment of tourist trinkets bedecked in shamrocks. Featured on a wire stand by the cash register were several books with lodging information as well as a booklet about Charles Fort itself. She added those to her pile of loot and paid the friendly young woman behind the counter.

Rachel slipped off her backpack and tucked the lodging books in. Those were research. She adjusted the pack and, booklet in hand, crossed the wooden bridge to the gateway as she read.

"Oof."

"Sorry." Rachel looked up from the detailed explanation of why the fort was star-shaped, cheeks on fire. Her eyes locked with familiar blue orbs sparkling with laughter. "Oh. It's you."

Colin's laugh rolled over her like an ocean wave. "Yep."

"What brings you out here?"

"Same as you, I imagine. Charles Fort, built in the late sixteen hundreds, is considered one of the finest existing specimens of a star fort, a wall configuration specifically designed to withstand canon fire."

"You've been reading the guide, I see." Rachel brandished her booklet and glanced at his hands.

He spread his fingers. "Nope. That's a direct quote from Patrick as he was urging me out the door this morning. The locals are mighty proud of their historic sites. And in this case, I can see why."

She turned, her gaze roving over the solid exterior walls, complete with guard enclosures at each of the star's points. A long, narrow building, intact except for the roof, filled one side, and an open area littered with paving stones housed several canons. "It's definitely in good shape. Especially since, according to the booklet, it was captured somewhat easily owing to a failure to enclose all the high ground."

"Ah, well. Nothing's perfect, I imagine. Still, between the cliffs and the walls, I imagine she put up a pretty good fight." Colin paused, fixing her with his direct gaze. "Mind if I tag along while you're exploring?"

Tingles started in her stomach and spread rapidly through her. How could he affect her so much with a simple look? She swallowed and shook her head, not trusting her voice.

"Thanks. So," he nodded at her booklet, "what's first?"

The long building turned out to be the former barracks. Inside, the floor was overgrown and was now a soft expanse of green grass. Not even a hint of the previous floor showed through. Had it been stone? Dirt? The guide didn't say. They passed several families on a guided tour of the fort, small children dashing ahead of their parents, older teens lagging behind with bored expressions and music players plugged in.

"Where do you suppose they're from?" Colin's head swiveled to follow the group.

Rachel frowned. "I thought I heard one family speaking Spanish. But another definitely looked American. People come to Ireland from all over...or didn't you read the tourism website before you came?"

He grinned. "'Fraid I skipped that. I knew where I wanted to be—my gran's stories wouldn't have let me go anywhere else. What about you? Why Ireland?"

"Like I said last night, my aunt is here."

His eyebrows lifted. "That's it? Your aunt and the B&B? No thirst for adventure? A yearning to rediscover your roots?"

Rachel scoffed. Adventure was the last thing she wanted. She wanted quiet and predictable. A place where everything happened on time, the way it was meant to. She'd had enough "adventure" to last a lifetime. But a man like Colin, someone who'd drop everything and just wander from town to town with no plans or guarantee of employment, would never understand.

"What?" Colin offered a hand as they climbed steep stone stairs to the top of the wall.

Even braced for it, the spark that zinged up her arm when she took his hand nearly made her jump. She glanced at him out of the corner of her eye. Didn't he feel it? He didn't act like he did. When they reached the top, she tugged her fingers loose and turned to look out over the bay. Sailboats dotted the water below, colorful sails full in the breeze.

Rachel took a deep breath of ocean air. "What must that be like? Zipping along the water…it must feel so free."

"Haven't you ever sailed?"

She kept her eyes fixed on the boats, though his gaze seared into her. "No. I've been white water rafting—didn't care for it—but never sailing."

"I saw a flyer for tours, you ought to take one while you're here."

Really? He was giving her touring advice? "I'll keep that in mind. I think I'll walk that way, see the rest of the battlements."

"Sounds like a plan."

Colin had followed her for the remainder of her explorations and then insisted on walking back to town with her. Rachel sighed and rubbed her feet. She'd enjoyed his company…when he wasn't being irritating. How could someone with no job and no plans to have one be so self-assured? Even now, when she had a firm goal and the beginning of a plan to achieve it, she had nowhere near that level of confidence. Flipping through the tourism books hadn't helped. Did every third family in Ireland rent out a room or two in their house? The listing of B&Bs in Kinsale alone was discouraging. This darling little town couldn't possibly get *that* many visitors each year, could it?

"Rachel, dear?" Her aunt knocked on the bedroom door before pushing it open. "Are you ready for supper? I thought we could go down to the Tire again, if you don't mind. I tend not to keep much on hand when we've no guests. Patrick's prices are reasonable enough that when it's just me, it's near about the same as shopping. Without all the hassle."

Rachel held in a sigh. She didn't want to see Colin again so soon. She'd get lost in those eyes, that voice…and he was leaving tomorrow. "I thought we were going to spend some time going over the books and how things run?"

"That'll keep 'til tomorrow now, won't it? We've no one staying and no one booked for the rest of the week." Siobhan came into the room and perched on the edge of the bed. "You're your father's daughter, I can see that about you. He was always dashing from one thing to the next with a firm plan and all the gumption it took to get him there. But it's no guarantee of health, wealth, and happiness, you know. And your father learned that the hard way, first with your mother, then with his own illness. You've got to trust that the Lord will provide in His time. And for Ireland, that means tourists in their season as well."

Rachel offered a slight smile. The guides all agreed that high season didn't begin until June, but back in the States travel websites all encouraged trips beginning as soon as April to take advantage of decent weather and off-season prices. "There were tour groups at the fort today though…"

Siobhan dismissed her words with a wave. "Sure and we've tourists year round. But in the off season, they're usually bus tours and they stay at the hotels in town. B&Bs cater to folks who travel on their own. We'll start getting more business in May or thereabout, don't fret. So as you see, there's plenty of time yet for you to decide what I'm doing wrong and make some changes."

"That's not…Aunt Siobhan, do you not want me here? I thought I was going to be a help to you."

"Oh, m'girl, of course I want you here. And where else would you go? You've no other family, nor do I. But you're young enough yet that you shouldn't be so focused on work that you miss the beauty around you." Siobhan stood and smoothed her slacks. "I'm guessing you can find enough to tide you by in the kitchen. But if you're wanting to come along down the pub with me, that's fine. I'll be heading out in a few minutes, and I'd love for you to join me."

5

Colin kept one eye on the door as he fiddled. Would she come again tonight? Even having spent the whole day with Rachel, it would be wonderful to have more time with her. Just knowing she was sitting there, listening to him play, would be enough. A few families came in with warm greetings for Patrick as he manned his station behind the bar. The kids clapped excitedly as they pointed to Colin and tugged on their parent's clothing, dragging them to tables closer to the music. Laughing, he added a flourish to the end of the jig, nodding his head to acknowledge the children's joy.

He let his gaze roam over the room, emptier than the previous night, being a weekday, but still full enough. Patrick did a brisk business with the locals. The few emails Colin had exchanged with his parents since he'd arrived in Ireland suggested they hadn't paid as much attention to Gran's stories as he had. They'd been appalled that families ate out at pubs. He'd tried to explain the difference between an Irish pub and a bar back home, but they couldn't see the distinction. He hadn't felt like continuing the argument, so he ignored further comments in their notes.

Colin reached behind him for his uilleann pipes. They were a gift from the owner of the first pub he'd worked in Dublin. The owner's son had given him a few lessons in the mornings before they had to start setting up for the lunch crowd. Colin snickered. Those first attempts had sounded like an injured wild animal in desperate need of being put down. He'd gotten better since then, but he needed plenty of practice, and perhaps a few more lessons, if he was ever going to be any good. This set of pipes was only a practice set, lacking the drones and regulators of a full set, but it required enough work that even after a month of concerted effort, he could manage only one song. Still, the haunting tones were so soft and lovely…it was worth the time spent practicing. Hopefully tonight's crowd wouldn't mind being the test audience for his efforts.

As he transitioned into the chorus, the door opened again. Rachel's aunt entered, scanned the room, then pulled herself onto a stool at the bar. The door closed and his heart sank. She wasn't going to come. Had he scared her away?

This morning he'd seen her heading down the road from the window in his bathroom. After he finished shaving, he'd gone downstairs to find something for breakfast. Patrick was there already, prepping for the day. He'd been happy enough to share the likely destination of one walking down that road, and Colin gave in easily enough to the suggestion that it was a sight worth seeing.

Even if the fort hadn't been, the hours spent with Rachel were worthwhile.

He thought back over their conversation. They'd had some spirited discussion—she was a woman who craved order, though she had a sense of adventure she didn't seem to be aware of. You didn't leave everything familiar to come to a foreign country unless you did. Rachel seemed to think it was the only logical decision. The corners of his mouth curved. She was adorable when she got fired up. It never occurred to her that the logical course of action was to get a roommate—she had mentioned four friends that sounded like reasonable possibilities to him—and find a job and move on with life right there where you knew people. Uprooting yourself from the place you'd been born and raised took guts. Why didn't she see that?

A smattering of applause greeted the end of the song. Colin grinned and inclined his head. He tucked the pipes behind his violin at the back of the small platform and hopped down. Time for a break. He paused here and there as he crossed the pub to chat with the families that greeted him. They were surprised he was an American, though on hearing his last name they smiled and inevitably commented that he was returning to his roots. At the bar, he slid onto the stool next to Rachel's aunt.

"'Evening."

Siobhan smiled. "You're very good with the pipes. Have you played long?"

35

Colin shook his head. "That's the only song I know. I'm just scratching the surface—but it's a marvelous instrument."

Patrick made his way down the length of the bar, wiping spills and taking orders as he did. He stopped in front of Colin. "Well done m'boy. Well done. What can I get you?"

"Do you have the potato soup again today?"

"Sure and we have that every day." Patrick grinned. "Brown bread to go along?"

"Yes, please. And a pot of tea?"

Patrick shook his head. "I'm all for tea, mind you, but you won't even try a Guinness?"

Colin chuckled. "No, sorry. I'll stick to my tea, but thanks."

Siobhan's eyes twinkled as shifted to look at Colin. "'Tis like refusing mother's milk not to at least try it."

"Ah, but I've been away from my mother for a good many years now." Colin winked. "Anyway, I sing better with a clear head and, well, I made a promise that I intend to keep."

"Well, and that's fine then." Siobhan nodded. "A promise is something we know about here. My niece mentioned you were out touring today as well. How did you enjoy our fort?"

Patrick brought a bowl of soup and small loaf of bread and set them in front of Colin. "Tea's on its way."

Colin broke a piece of bread off and dunked it in the thick soup. "It's a lovely place—you can almost feel the soldiers still marching around. If you close your eyes and let yourself, you can hear them stomping in formation."

Siobhan's smile widened to a grin. "That's a fine way of putting it. You've enough Irish left in you, I'd wager. Not so sure about me niece."

"Oh?" He waved his thanks to Patrick for the pot of tea that appeared by his plate and poured the steaming liquid into a mug.

"She's a good girl, but she seems scared of life. Maybe losing both your parents and your home in so short a time will do that, but she's so focused on work. I had to practically kick her out of the house this morning. She's holed up at home with the records for the last two years and nothing I could say would budge her, for all that she came back this afternoon with Colin this and Colin that."

His heart skipped a beat but he forced his face to remain impassive, save for a twitch of a smile at the corner of his lips. "I enjoyed her company—I'm glad to know she had fun as well. I'd wondered."

Siobhan shook her head. "That girl. Well, you'll be around for a bit, won't you? A friend might be just what she needs."

"Actually..." Colin scooped the last of his soup. "I'll be moving on tomorrow. Though I'm planning to stay in County Cork for a while, so who knows? Maybe Rachel and I will run into one another again."

Siobhan's shoulders slumped but she said nothing.

"I'd best get back to my singing—got to be sure I pay for my supper."

Dense fog rolled in off the bay, shrouding everything. Colin checked in the bathroom one last time before throwing his hiking-style backpack over one shoulder and clomping down the stairs.

"Off then, are ya'?" Patrick stopped chopping potatoes and wiped his hands on the apron tied around his waist.

"Yep. I loaded up my instruments already. They're the only reason I bought that clunker out there. But she gets me where I'm going, and that's all I can ask." The second-hand car had also served as a bed on the odd nights when he hadn't been able to find a spot to play and had left it too long to get a room at an inn. He'd learned to start looking before supper-time. Apparently B&Bs tended to close up earlier in the off-season, and not every town had a more traditional hotel.

"Well then, I hope we'll see you back again before long. I'll always have room for you, should you want it."

Colin gripped Patrick's extended hand, laughing when the old man pulled him into a back-slapping hug. "Thanks. For everything."

Patrick nodded and returned to his chopping. Colin let out a breath and pushed through the swinging door that separated the kitchen from the main pub. Emptiness filled him. It was time to leave though. Entanglements of any kind simply weren't in his plans. Not yet. His heart still hadn't healed from the slashes Jessica had ripped through it. Besides, if his experience in Chicago had taught him anything, it was that he was no good at relationships. If he had been, he surely would have seen it coming.

Colin tossed his backpack into the passenger seat and rounded the car. It sputtered to life with a cough and a bang and a cloud of smoke from the muffler. He should get that looked at. Maybe in the next town. He wound around through Kinsale, with one final, lingering look at the darkened windows of the Sea Haven B&B. Would she miss him even a tiny bit?

The mist congealed into rain. It wasn't a hard rain, more like excess water finding there was nothing to do but fall. The locals called it "soft weather." It was an apt term. Walking in it wasn't bad, but driving was a challenge. You didn't quite need the wipers, but you couldn't quite do without them, either. So you either dealt with an annoying squeak every third wipe or you spent half your time manually clearing droplets from the windshield. Irish drivers didn't appear to even notice the wet roads. They zipped around him at speeds well over the posted limit. If there was room, Colin slid to the side when he saw them coming. The gravel shoulder crunched under his tires. But at least this time there weren't bushes reaching out with scrabbling arms to scratch the car.

What should have been a forty minute drive to Blarney took close to twice that. He turned down the wrong road once, which cost him some time but gained him an up close encounter with a cow that had nothing better to do than stand in the middle of the road and moo. More than likely, he could have made that detour work, but waiting for a bovine to decide to move wasn't high on his list of exciting pastimes. After that adventure, he needed a cup of tea and a snack. Then maybe he'd take a stroll around, see the castle, and find out if the town of Blarney might not be the perfect spot to stay a day or two.

6

"Did you have a nice evening last night?" Rachel brought her coffee to the kitchen table and settled across from her aunt.

"I did, yes. It's always lovely to spend a few hours with friends. I had a nice chat with that American boy as well. What was his name?"

Heat stole across Rachel's cheeks as Colin's face flashed into her mind. "Colin. He's leaving today. Probably already gone."

"So he said." Siobhan fixed Rachel in a long look. "He seemed disappointed that you didn't come by."

Rachel shrugged, though her heart leapt. Had he enjoyed their time together that much? The corners of his mouth were always turned up in a smile, so it was hard to tell. "I appreciate you letting me stay and look things over. There's nothing to change, really."

"Oh?" A smile flirted with the curves of Siobhan's lips. "Everything's in order then?"

Rachel sighed and sipped her coffee. "Yes. And I'm sorry I've been a pain about it. Finding that Dad's business was in such bad shape after having assumed it was fine—being *told* it was fine—for so long…"

"Not to worry. But you see now why I'm not concerned. We do well enough. With April just around the bend, bookings will pick up and you'll have ample opportunity to earn your keep." Siobhan smiled, taking the sting from her words. "In the meantime, you should go see the sights while they're less crowded and you've the energy to do it. Once we start having guests every night, you'll be aching for some time to yourself."

It seemed like she'd only had time to herself lately. Well, herself and her dad's lawyer. But her aunt had a point. When her dad's cabins had been rented out year-round, there had been precious little time for relaxation. Hospitality wasn't an industry to get into if you liked your nights and weekends to yourself. But even knowing that, it'd be the only thing that interested Rachel. Must be in the blood. "All right. What do you suggest?"

"Go up and see Blarney Castle. Kiss the stone. See about getting a bit of that gift of gab into you. And don't forget to browse the woolen mills while you're there. If you see something you like, make a note, many of our local craftspeople can do the same work for much less."

Rachel chuckled and finished her coffee. "A castle sounds like just the thing. The fort yesterday was nice, but it's more like a ruin. I'll head out after breakfast. Do you want to come?"

Siobhan shook her head. "You go ahead."

Rachel turned off the engine and sighed, flexing her hands. She hadn't gripped a steering wheel that hard since she was first learning to drive. But at least she hadn't actually hit anyone. The square castle speared into the sky, a smaller round tower beside it. It wasn't an imposing sight—certainly nothing like Cinderella's castle or Buckingham Palace—though both of those were modern compared to this.

Passing through the Visitor's Center, Rachel purchased a booklet about the castle. The tourism board certainly did a good job giving visitors information. She flipped to the first page and skimmed the basic information. Built in 1210...wow. Tucking the booklet in her backpack, Rachel strode down the path toward the structure. The grounds were lovely—already lush and green— she'd have to spend some time wandering after she toured the building.

Nearing the foot of the castle, Rachel stretched her neck and looked toward the top. It hadn't looked so tall from the parking lot. Following the gravel path and brown arrows, she found the entrance to the keep and climbed the stairs. Stooping to get through the archway into the first room she sighed. Not, in fact, an intact castle. That explained her aunt's grin. She tugged the pamphlet from her backpack and studied the drawn map more closely. Signs with arrows directed her across to another archway if she wanted to see the Blarney Stone. She was here…might as well.

More stairs greeted her when she ducked through the arch. The passage was narrow; her elbows practically touching either side as she climbed. Hopefully you went down a different way. A break in the wall led her into the second main area of the keep—the description in the guide said it was most likely for family living. There was very little actual floor, so she hugged the wall and continued around to the next set of stairs. Glancing up she saw plenty of sky.

The rest of the trip to the top was the same. Dark, narrow stairs around the outside of the gutted castle keep. Rachel paused at each level to read her booklet and learn about the suspected uses of each different floor. Thank the Lord she'd been born in modern times. Though did you know how hard it was if you had no other point of reference, or was it simply the way things were?

A beam of sunlight pierced the clouds as she sidled through an archway and found herself on the battlements. She scooted toward the edge. Breathtaking. Miles of green stretched out in all directions. There was a small forested area nearby—that had to be part of the castle grounds—as well as a garden, already a riot of color. Beyond that, fields and towns, and dozens of white dots that had to be sheep. The sweetness of the air filled her lungs as she breathed deeply. Even though they weren't on the best of terms right now, Rachel could admit that God outdid Himself when He made Ireland. She picked her way around the edge of the keep, taking in the panoramic views, each new vista more impressive than the last.

As Rachel made her way around the battlements, a young man with a shock of flaming red hair and freckles across his nose stood. "'Morning. Come to kiss the stone then, have ya'?"

"Does it really give you the gift of gab?" Rachel fought the urge to roll her eyes. She'd come here at her aunt's urging, but hadn't actually intended to kiss any stones. But…she was here, and really, wasn't it something you had to do if you came to Ireland?

Another young man ducked through the arch labeled "Exit" and grinned. "Sure and it does. Centuries of Irishmen wouldn't lie now, would they?"

Rachel blinked, looking between the two young men. They laughed in unison.

"Aye, we're twins. Ma says it was a right surprise when we came out. She'd been hoping for a girl at last, ya see. But here we come, not one, but two more boys to add to her brood." The first young man spoke, nudging his brother with his elbow.

She cleared her throat. "Brood?"

The other jumped in, a laugh in his voice. "We're six and seven, the pair of us. Ruined her even number as well. Been causing trouble ever since, if you listen to Ma."

Rachel chuckled. "So…where's this stone I'm supposed to kiss?"

The red-heads exchanged a glance before nodding toward a pair of iron bars bolted into the battlements. In unison, they both stepped into a hole by the wall and sat. "D'you have a camera?"

Rachel nodded and tugged the camera out of her pack, handing it to one of the brothers.

"Great, just drop your backpack and then sit here, facing the middle of the keep." The first patted the edge of the roof.

Her eyebrows lifting, Rachel did as instructed. "Okay…now what?"

"Now you lie back and grab the bars, don't worry, we'll help and steady you. As you lean back, you'll see the stone. Give 'er a big smooch, wait for your photo, and we'll help you back up."

A herd of grasshoppers began jumping in her belly as she cast a sideways glance at the boys. Did she really want to lean out over nothingness just to kiss a rock? "Um…"

"Ah come now, 'tisn't bad. Here we are then." The man on her right pressed gently on her shoulder, and she leaned back. Swallowing the bile that crept up her throat, Rachel reached back and gripped the bars. Cold sweat swamped her, causing her fingers to slip. She squeezed the bars harder.

"There you go. Just a tiny bit farther…and kiss."

Rachel's head dropped back. She saw the ground far below her, just a few widely spaced bars and her grip the only things separating her from a gruesome death. Her vision blurred and the earth seemed to spin. Stomach churning, she squeezed her eyes closed and puckered up, her lips brushing the cold, moist rock.

There was a flash of light and voices began speaking from miles away.

"...Miss?"

She opened her eyes and forced herself to raise her head.

"Sit up now, nice and easy."

The brothers each took an arm and helped her to sit. She leaned forward and cradled her head in her hands.

"Are you alright then?" Furrows etched the man's brow as he offered her camera.

"Yeah. Yeah, I'm fine." Rachel stood, brushing her hands on her pants. "But that's definitely a once in a lifetime experience."

They chuckled. "Enjoy your stay. The stairs down are just over there."

"Thanks." She hooked her backpack over one shoulder and, praying her legs wouldn't give out, headed toward the exit sign.

There were new rooms to investigate on the way down, little nooks off to the side of the staircases that had been used for storage or sleeping but were now plain and empty stone spaces. Stepping through the final archway, Rachel let out a breath. Solid ground at last. She walked around to the front of the castle and sank onto a bench. She'd just rest a minute and try to erase the sensation of her life flashing before her eyes.

"You didn't really kiss the stone, did you?"

Rachel's eyes flew open. Colin stood in front of her, a smile playing at the corners of his mouth. Her stomach fluttered, an entirely different feeling than she'd had at the top of the keep.

"What are you doing here?"

"Same as you, I imagine. You can't come to Ireland without seeing the Blarney Stone." He nodded to the bench. "Can I join you?"

She scooted to make room. "Didn't you kiss the stone too, then?"

He sat and shook his head. "I went up and had a look, but there's no way I'm putting my mouth on that thing. They say the locals go up at night and pee on it you know."

She fought the urge to scrub at her mouth. He was joking, wasn't he? He had to be. "Did you lean out, at least?"

"Nope. I'm not afraid of much, but falling to my death? That's way up there." Colin cocked his head to the side. "What prompted you to drive out to Blarney today?"

"My aunt suggested it. She said I'm not talkative enough to be Irish. I guess they don't breed introverts here." Rachel grinned.

"Hmm. Any idea if your aunt talked to Patrick this morning?"

"No. Why?"

"Nothing. Just wondering." He drummed his fingers on his knee for a moment. "I was going to wander the grounds. I'd love it if you'd join me."

Warmth spread through her. "I'd like that. The rock close sounds particularly interesting."

"As long as we can tour the poison garden as well."

She arched a brow. "Poison garden?"

"It's a new feature—poisonous plants from around the globe all grown conveniently in one place."

"And who are you poisoning?"

He chuckled. "No one. But honestly, how can you resist the idea?"

It was an interesting thought—much like the carnivorous plants that so many people grew. "All right. I think I've recovered from my experience with the stone enough that I can walk again."

They consulted the map on her brochure and started down the path that would lead them through the rock close and to the gardens.

Rachel watched him out of the side of her eye for several minutes as they walked. He certainly seemed at ease with silence. Or at least lack of conversation. Birds were chirping and a stream chuckled somewhere nearby. It was peaceful. So why was her heart racing? She glanced up through her lashes. Handsome seemed too tame a word—Colin was one of God's finest specimens. How was it possible he was content to just wander with no plans, no guarantee of dinner the next day?

"Do you have a new spot lined up for tonight?"

Colin looked at her and shook his head. "Not yet. Though I noted a few possibilities as I drove into town. It's early yet to be asking. This afternoon's soon enough."

She drew her eyebrows together. "It doesn't bother you? Having no guarantees?"

His laugh startled a pair of birds in the tree overhead and they took off, squawking. "There are never any guarantees. Thinking you have them, relying on them…that's the quickest way to get blindsided and left in the dust."

"Okay, sure, things can happen, obviously. But if you plan, you work hard, you establish yourself…you end up with a solid, comfortable living. That's just the way the world works."

Colin stopped, shoving his hands in his pockets. "Not always. Look…before I came here I was the CEO of a software company in Chicago. Some college friends and I started it just out of school. For ten years we struggled, paid our dues, and finally got enough traction to start doing more than living paycheck to paycheck. But not everyone could handle the ups and downs—by last year, it was down to just two of the original founders. And then she—Jessica—made a deal behind my back and I was out. If you'd asked me if I was worried about something going wrong even the day before it went down I would've laughed at you. Now? Guarantees aren't worth the paper they're written on."

What did you say to that? Hurt, edging on bitterness, oozed through his words. "I'm sorry."

He shrugged. "Maybe it's an extreme reaction to leave the country and become a traveling musician, but I couldn't come up with any better ideas and I find I'm enjoying it more than I dreamed possible."

"Maybe in this case you're right. Sometimes a change is the right thing." She just wasn't sure about the lack of a plan. She met his gaze and offered a smile.

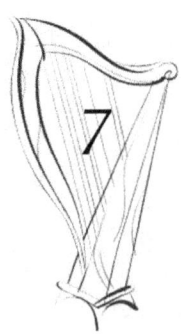

7

Colin kept his hands in his pockets as they began to walk again. His fingers itched to twine with hers, but that wasn't likely to go over very well. What was it about her that drew him? She was unlike anyone he'd ever dated—was that it? Jessica…well, it was probably better not to think about her.

"What's your favorite thing in Ireland so far?" Rachel stopped in front of a rock formation and tilted her head to the side as she looked at it.

Colin pulled his attention away from Rachel's shapely figure and eyed the rocks. Was that a witch stirring a pot? "Did these form naturally, or were they carved?"

Rachel consulted her booklet. "Hm. Combination, it seems. But you didn't answer my question."

He chuckled. "It's hard to say. There's always something amazing wherever I am at the time. Right now, this rock close is pretty amazing. Though I suspect when we make it to the poison garden, the wonders of mysterious, dangerous plants might slip into first place. After all, it's not often you get to see castor beans growing alongside mandrake and opium."

She shook her head. "Come on, now. Think harder. There's been no standout? You started in Dublin, right? The Book of Kells wasn't amazing?"

"Oh, it was delightful. And the library at Trinity College is incredible as well. But then, so's the drive through the Wicklow mountains or the cliffs along the southern coast like the ones Charles Fort was built on. Then you have the expansive fields of unbroken green and the towns that all pride themselves on keeping their streets and homes neat as a pin in hopes of winning the Tidy Town award...how do you choose?" Colin's grin spread. "Better to just enjoy each as you encounter it, don't you think?"

"Huh." Rachel gave him a long look before continuing down the path that wound through the rocks.

Colin followed in her wake. What was she thinking? Was there some reason she couldn't just enjoy things as they came?

"I guess that goes along with your whole 'see where the road leads you' philosophy."

He lifted a brow. She'd never injected that much scorn into her voice before. He cleared his throat. "It does. And speaking of that, I should probably start my hunt for a place to sing tonight, or book a room at a B&B. So I'll leave you to your wandering."

"Colin..." She sighed and pushed her bangs out of her eyes. "I'm sorry. Please stay."

"You're sure? I don't want to make you uncomfortable…and that's what seems to be happening."

"I'm sure."

He nodded and closed the distance between them. Sunlight washed across the end of the path up ahead. They must be near the end of the rock close. "It's not a permanent situation you realize, right?"

"What isn't?"

"The wandering. I can't say as I have a definite end date in mind, but it's not as if I plan to do this forever." His money would run out at some point. It wasn't an immediate concern, he'd made enough in the sale of his half of the company that it would be years at his current rate before it was an issue. Probably best not to mention that though.

She flashed a smile and stepped out into a clearing. "Looks like that's the way to the kitchen garden, and the poison garden is…" Rachel glanced down at the map and pointed to her right. "That way."

"What can I get you?" The server gave Colin and Rachel a cheerful smile from behind a glass case.

Colin eyed the quiches on display, saliva filling his mouth. He'd never been one for quiche 'til he came here. Now…he couldn't get enough. "I'll have a slice of the Lorraine and a pot of tea, please. Rachel?"

"That sounds good, actually. I'll have the same."

Colin waited as the girl behind the counter rang up the total and quickly offered his money before Rachel could object. The tea shop had been his idea, so it only seemed fair that he pay. Plus, this way he could count it as a date, even if she probably wouldn't.

"Go ahead and have a seat, I'll bring your food right out."

Colin scanned the small, empty seating area and nodded toward a table for two in the corner. "How about over there?"

Rachel shrugged. "Sure. And thanks, by the way. You didn't have to buy me lunch."

He grinned and pulled out a chair, gesturing for her to sit. "But I wanted to."

"Well, thanks."

"You said that already." He winked. "Now you've seen Charles Fort and Blarney. What else do you plan to see while you're here?"

"That's actually two more places than I'd originally planned to visit. I came to help Aunt Siobhan, not sightsee. Turns out she doesn't really need me though. I'm beginning to think she only invited me to come because she felt sorry for me. She made it sound like her business was barely scraping by, but now that I've looked things over…she doesn't need me."

"I'm sure that's not true. I don't know your aunt well, but I can't imagine she'd invite you to come if she wasn't happy about the prospect. Maybe she's sorry for you, too, but that's as it should be when someone you love has just lost their dad." Rachel probably wouldn't appreciate knowing his own heart hurt for her…best keep that tidbit to himself.

"I guess. But I'd started to map it all out, you know? Spend the summer helping Aunt Siobhan, then over the winter we could work out a transition plan and by next year, she could be retired and I'd have taken over for her. Everyone wins. Now…I'm not even sure if I'll stay past July. And if I go back, then what?" Her shoulders sagged.

The server appeared at the table with two steaming slices of quiche and two small silver tea kettles. "Here you go. Let me know if you need anything else."

Colin breathed in the rich eggy scent. Earthy undertones hinted at mushrooms hidden within the enormous slice of quiche. A small salad hugged the edge of the plate, adding some color to the generous helping of food. He tipped the kettle into his cup before stirring in some milk and sugar. Rachel's eyes bored into him. He paused with his fork hovering over the tip of his quiche. "What?"

"I just thought you'd want to bless the meal…the other night…"

"I wasn't sure you'd want me to." He grasped her hand. The expected sparks that bit his fingers as they twined with hers, and he said a short prayer over the food. He loosened his hold but didn't pull his hand away. She left her hand in his. Did she feel it too? Colin cleared his throat. "So, if you go back to the States, where's home?"

Rachel stabbed at her plate. "I don't know. There's nothing left for me in the Virginia mountains. Maybe a few friends, but they're all married and moving on with the lives. Most of them left for college and never came back, anyway."

"So you could choose anywhere—clean slate? That could be exciting."

She shrugged. "I guess. But that's why I chose Kinsale. And at least here I have family, well, for as long as Aunt Siobhan's around anyway."

"I get that…but hasn't there been somewhere you've always wanted to live, or at least visit?" He could list four or five places in the US that he'd like to try out. Was he that unusual?

Rachel pursed her lips and tapped her fork against her plate. "Maybe. I haven't really thought about it. My plan was to help Dad with the cabins then take over after he retired. But with all the medical bills…there was nothing to do but sell. If I'm not needed here…I guess I'll have to spend some time figuring that out."

Colin watched the tail lights of Rachel's car disappear behind bushes that reached out into the road, separating lush fields from pavement and doing a semi-decent job of keeping the sheep from wandering into traffic. His lips stretched into a smile. What a great way to spend an afternoon. After their lunch, Rachel had tagged along as he visited a few of the pubs and restaurants along the main street in Blarney and asked about a night or two of music in exchange for a place to stay. She'd seemed surprised that he'd found someplace as easily as he did. In fact, he'd had enough interest that he was planning to stay in the area for a week and split his time between three different venues. Blarney was a central location and he could make a few day trips and explore a bit more of the countryside without needing to change lodgings. And he could always zip down to Kinsale and see how Rachel was faring.

He shook his head, tucked his hands in his pockets and ambled toward the pub where he'd be playing later that night. The owner had a storage room behind the kitchen and had offered to bring over a cot. It wasn't fancy, but it'd certainly do well enough. And if it didn't, he could go ahead and book a room in a local B&B. Either way, he'd still play. It was a nice way to pass the evening.

"You're here then, are ye?" The pub owner looked up from polishing glasses behind a long, dark wood bar that ran the length of the room on one side.

"I am. I left my car around back like you said. Can I help you with anything, or should I just stay out of the way?"

The man grinned, jerking his head toward the swinging door in the corner. "I've got your cot set up in the back, if you wanted to rest a bit, that'd be fine."

Colin nodded. He could take a hint. He pushed through the door into the kitchen. Pots bubbled and pans sizzled on the stove manned by a young man wearing an apron. They exchanged nods, and Colin continued through the space. He poked his head through a doorway and smiled. A single bed was set up against the shelves on one side of the room. Blankets were stretched tight and held in place with precise corners.

Turning back into the kitchen, he pursed his lips. The owner had said there was an exit to the parking lot behind the pub. But where was the door? It had to be somewhere near here. Aha. He turned the knob on a door partially hidden by aprons and brooms and pushed. Sure enough, there was his car. He clicked the unlock button on the key fob and opened the trunk. Warmth filled him as his gaze landed on his instruments. Other than a few boxes he'd stored with his parents before coming to Ireland, they were the bulk of his possessions. He gathered them, and his backpack, and nudged the trunk closed with his elbow.

Back in the storage room, he carefully laid the instruments on the floor before stretching onto the cot. He tugged his mobile phone out of his pocket and opened up the email program. There were a few notes from old friends and business contacts, one from his mom, and...Jessica? His breath caught and a lead weight settled in his stomach. What did she want? Did he even want to know? Colin took a deep breath and opened Jessica's message.

Hey Colin,

Just thought I'd check in and see how your little vacation was going. Ready to come back yet? I only ask because a few of the new board members have asked—seems they were under the impression that we were both staying after the sale. I tried to explain that no one has ever been able to make you do anything. Still, they're wondering when you'll be returning. There's talk of

opening a Federal systems group in the DC area and they want
you to head it up.

Let me know what I should tell them.

-Jess

He shook his head. What should she tell them? There weren't polite words for what she could tell them, though it wasn't really the new board's fault. They'd dealt with a viper when they set up the deal, one who was willing to take advantage of the loose legal definitions in their corporate structure to go behind his back and cut him out of the loop. Jessica had expected him to stay and simply deal with it. How had she not realized that wasn't going to happen? In all, it wasn't a terrible arrangement, but they hadn't needed it. The company was doing fine without investors and a supervisory board. Now they wanted to branch into government contracting? Well, good luck to them. He'd cashed out and wasn't going back. He deleted the message and scrolled down, scanning the senders. Might as well see what Mom had to say, then it'd be time to go get set up.

8

"How was your trip yesterday?" Siobhan leaned against the door frame of the guest room.

Rachel looked up from scrubbing the edge of the bathroom floor and sat back on her heels. "Good. Though I would've appreciated a warning about the Blarney Stone itself."

Rich laughter tumbled from her aunt. "Now where'd be the fun in that?"

Rachel shook her head and swiped a sponge across the last bit of tile before pushing to her feet. She grabbed the bucket full of soapy water and dropped the sponge into it. "We're all set in here for our guest tonight."

"We were before, though a nice fresh wash never hurt a floor." Siobhan angled her head, her eyes fixed on Rachel. "But you're changing the subject."

Sighing, Rachel slipped past her aunt and headed down the stairs. In the kitchen, she emptied the bucket into the sink and began rinsing the sponge, her mind a jumble.

"Well?" Siobhan lowered herself into a chair.

Rachel squeezed the sponge and dropped it onto the dish rack to dry. Wiping her hands on a towel, she crossed the room and sat across from her aunt. "Did you know he was going to be there?"

The wrinkles in her aunt's forehead deepened as she drew her eyebrows together. "Who?"

"Colin. From the Flat Tire?"

"Was he now? No, I'd no idea he'd gone in that direction." A smile ghosted across her lips. "Though I imagine that made your time more pleasant…and it explains your late arrival home."

Rachel frowned. She'd arrived home late because she'd gotten lost. Twice. It didn't matter that the guidebooks said there were no wrong roads in Ireland, when you wanted to get back to dinner and a warm bed, the longer, scenic route wasn't the preferred one. "It was nice enough. I guess. Though…"

Her aunt stood and turned on the fire under the kettle on the stove. "I'll make some tea. I've always found it easier to talk with a nice hot cuppa at my side."

Rachel watched as Siobhan fixed a pot of tea and brought it to the table, along with two cups and a small plate of cookies.

"Now then, have a biscuit and some tea and tell me about it."

There wasn't much to tell. Still, maybe it would help to talk about it. She helped herself to a cookie and nibbled the edge.

"There's nothing to tell, honestly. I like being around him, it's...comfortable? Maybe that's not the right word but I can't come up with a better one. And yet...he's perfectly content to have no job. No steady income. He just moves from place to place when the whim strikes. How is that possible? Why doesn't he worry about having enough money for gas? Or lunch? What if something happened and he needed medical care? There are so many things that could go wrong before he realized it was happening and it's as if he doesn't even know that. How can he not know that?"

Siobhan wrapped her fingers around her teacup, slight tremors making ripples in the steaming liquid. "The only guarantee we have in this life is that we'll be with Jesus at the end of it if we've made the decision to trust Him. You know that, don't you?"

Rachel grimaced. "Of course I do. But that doesn't mean you should just skip through life without a plan. And a backup plan. And maybe a few extra hundred dollars stashed away for a rainy day. Because, guaranteed or not, it's as likely to rain on you as anything else."

"Oh, sweetheart." Siobhan laid her hand on Rachel's. "That's why I wanted you to come for a while. You've had more than your share of heartache in your life, especially for one so young. But you can't let it turn you into someone who's scared to cross the street."

"Wanting to have a place to call home and a steady income isn't the same thing as being afraid." Was she the only one who saw how silly it was for a grown man to flit around a foreign country like a backpacking teenager? "It's not as if a career in hospitality—particularly one based on tourism—doesn't have its insecurity. But it's predictable, to a degree. And you can plan for those low season doldrums."

Siobhan nodded. "I suppose that's true, so far as it goes. But there's plenty else in life that you can't plan or predict. And you're happier, overall, when you stop trying so hard to control it all."

Frowning, Rachel set her cookie—or biscuit, as her aunt called it—down beside her tea. Maybe she had a point. Her father had been a planner, as had her mom. And yet they'd still died young, leaving her alone with a mountain of debt that she'd only gotten out from under by selling her home. So what, really, had all those plans gained them? Or her?

Rachel collapsed onto her bed with a sigh. The family staying the night had, finally, returned to their room after an evening in the guest lounge. Aunt Siobhan had encouraged Rachel to spend some time with them, chatting and making sure they were comfortable. Though she'd tried to suggest various activities within walking distance, they'd been content to settle on the sofa and talk while the kids pulled board games out of Siobhan's well-stocked cabinet. Her stomach rumbled, reminding Rachel that she hadn't had time for dinner. She should get up and make a sandwich...or she could just wait 'til breakfast.

There was a tap at the door, then Siobhan poked her head in. "Still awake?"

"Yeah. Though I was just thinking about calling it a night. Do they need something?"

Siobhan shook her head and entered the room with a tray. "I brought you some food. Nothing fancy, but I thought since you missed supper you might be hungry."

Rachel grinned and sat up, patting the bed. "You're a mind reader. I'd talked myself out of looking for something to eat."

Siobhan chuckled. "There's time enough for skipping meals when we're busy. One family—especially one with such well-behaved children—is no reason to go hungry." She set the tray on Rachel's bed and perched on the nearby chair. "Tell me about them."

If her aunt had wanted to get to know them, why had she gone down to the pub and left Rachel alone for the evening? Whatever. She picked up the thick sandwich and took a bite. Roast beef and the sharp white cheddar that was unique to Ireland on thick, homemade bread. Yum. "They're from Kansas, Sherri and Jim. They met in high school and haven't left their hometown other than their honeymoon to the gulf shores. So their daughter, Ellie, she's the older child, has been reading Yeats in school, fell in love with his poems, and convinced her parents that they needed to come and see the island that inspired him."

"That's charming. Imagine going so far out of your comfort zone for your child simply because she asked."

Rachel nodded. Her parents would have done the same, if they'd been able to scrape the money together and find someone to mind the resort. That was one of the major downsides to owning a vacation site, it was hard to get your own time off. They'd done a good deal of traveling during the off season within the U.S., but going overseas had always been just out of reach.

"How long are they here, then?"

"A month. Jim saved up his vacation days for more than a year so they'd have a long time to see every square corner of the country. His words." Rachel dabbed the corner of her mouth with the napkin and took a sip of her water. "How was the pub, and Patrick?"

Pink tinged her aunt's cheeks. "Everyone's fine. They're missing your young man, though. Patrick's got the recorded music playing, but it's not the same. I imagine he'll have a fine crowd on the weekend for his live musician. We got spoiled."

"He's not my young man, Aunt Siobhan."

"Aye, but he could be, I think. Don't focus so hard on what was or you'll lose sight of what could be. You don't want to end up looking back over your life with regrets." Siobhan stood and reached for the tray. "Now, go on to bed. We'll start breakfast at seven and you'll want to be showered and dressed before the guests are up and about."

Rachel nodded. "Thanks for the sandwich. 'Night."

Siobhan kissed the top of Rachel's head and carried the tray from the room. The door clicked shut and Rachel lay back on her pillows. What had her aunt meant about regrets? Had there been something she could have done to make things work out between her and Patrick? If their faith is what kept them apart…how did you fix that?

The family from Kansas had seemed nice, like people she'd be friends with, given the chance, but they'd brought on a touch of homesickness. How could she miss something she didn't have though? Home…that had been her parents. Tears filled her eyes and her breath caught in her chest. She'd done what had to be done, so why was she still crying over it? Once Mom and Dad were both gone, the cabins were just another place to be. Where was home going to be now?

Rachel flopped onto her side and stared at the closed door of her room. The inn, her aunt, they were supposed to be her new home. But Siobhan didn't need her. Didn't even really seem to want her long-term. Oh sure, she was happy Rachel had come for a visit, but would she even consider letting her stay? She'd spent some time looking at Ireland's immigration policies. Staying more permanently would be hard, but it wasn't impossible. And that was what she wanted, wasn't it? To put down roots, find a new place to call home.

Colin's face floated through her mind and her aunt's words echoed. Could he be her "young man"? Did she even want him to be? He was certainly nice to look at—attraction wasn't the problem. And she had enough experience with guys to be pretty confident he felt it, too. He was smart, and if his prayers before meals were anything to go on, had a solid relationship with God. More solid than hers, most likely. She was working on that, but it was a challenge. After all, had God really needed to take both her parents and the resort? Where was the purpose in that? Siobhan insisted He had one but, well, Rachel wasn't convinced.

Still…Colin hit all the items on her list. Well, all but one. Steady employment. Security. Rachel sighed. With all the checks in the plus column and only one in the minus…maybe she could let go long enough to explore the possibilities.

9

Colin tucked his duffel bag in snug with his instruments and shut the car's trunk. The week in Blarney had been profitable. He'd enjoyed moving from pub to pub but still being, roughly, in the same place. A few of the locals had even changed from their usual haunts to follow him when he changed locations. He smiled. There was no word other than gratifying. It was a little hard to leave. And yet…there was so much more to see. So why had he spent the morning plotting various routes back to Kinsale?

He'd allowed himself to hope, or at least half-hope, that Rachel would come and hear him play. She'd left with his itinerary. And his phone number. And email address. Nothing. Why hadn't he asked for a way to contact her? The B&B. Before he could talk himself out of it, Colin dug his wallet out of his pocket and flipped through the scraps of paper and business cards. A quick call to Patrick got him the number for the B&B. He took a deep breath and punched the numbers.

"Sea Haven Bed and Breakfast. How can I help you?"

Colin's lips curved up. Rachel sounded so professional and she even had a hint of an Irish lilt in her voice. "Hi, there. Um. It's Colin."

"Oh, hi. How are you?"

Colin boosted himself up on the back of his car. "Good. Just packing up to leave Blarney. It's been a good week and it was nice to be in one place for a little bit."

"Really? I would've thought that'd cramp your style."

He let out a short laugh. "Less than you'd imagine. How are things there?"

"Picking up. We've had at least one room booked each night. One day we were actually fully booked. Aunt Siobhan runs a tight ship...and has everything firmly under control." Rachel sighed, her breath crackling in the earpiece of the phone.

"And...that's a bad thing?" Colin frowned as he looked out across the square that occupied the center of Blarney. A group of kids was gathering, several with soccer balls tucked under an arm.

"No. No, of course it's not. I'm just...I thought she needed me to help her. That this was supposed to be my next step. Now it's looking like I'll be on that flight back to the States in another month. And then what am I supposed to do?"

Colin's heart ached at the sorrow in her voice. Was there anything he could do to help? Nothing sprang immediately to mind. "I'm sorry."

"Thanks. I'm wishing I had a little of your happy-go-lucky right about now. Maybe then the prospect of ending up where I started with nothing to show for it wouldn't sting quite so much."

He winced. Was there any point in trying to explain that he cared about what happened next, he just wasn't going to waste time worrying about it? Probably not. It was pretty clear she'd made up her mind about him. Which made this phone call—and all the time he spent thinking about Rachel—a waste. "Okay then. I guess I'll let you go. You probably have rooms to turn over, that sort of thing."

Colin hit the end button as Rachel started to speak and reined in his wayward thoughts. He was two for two in choosing wrong when it came to thinking he might have found the right woman— did he not understand how to hear the Holy Spirit at all? First, there was Jessica…though admittedly he hadn't been overly concerned about the Holy Spirit then. They'd gone to a Christian college together and he'd thought that was enough evidence of shared beliefs. Boy had he been wrong about that. Then he'd taken all that new understanding and tossed it out the window when Rachel came along, falling right back into the same rut. Physical and intellectual attraction were there in spades, and Colin liked the glimpses of spirituality he'd seen, too. But, just like Jessica, Rachel didn't respect him or his choices.

With a sigh, he slid off the back of the car. Time to move on.

Colin checked that the disc from the machine at the corner where you paid to park was visible through his windshield and turned, looking down the street lined with shops, cafes, and pubs. The buildings on the main street of Cork city were three and four stories high—were there apartments above or did the shops own those spaces as well? Probably a mixture. People bustled down the sidewalks, tourists ambled, mouths ajar as they took in the sights. He smiled and tucked his hands into his pockets. Did he look like a tourist or someone who belonged?

The sign for the English Market caught his eye. Might as well grab a bite to eat before continuing his search for a place to play for a bit. None of the towns on the way to Cork from Blarney had netted him a gig, but surely there'd be something in the city proper. Even if he couldn't find a place to play, that didn't mean he had to go running back to the States. He could afford to be a pure tourist for a while and, if that got boring, look into finding a tech job. He had the skills and Ireland had enough of a burgeoning technology industry…he could probably make it work. And if not…well, there was a whole world out there. He gave himself a firm mental shake. Rachel's criticism of his choices stung, but there wasn't a correlation between them and this situation. Nor was it a portent of the end of his ability to make a living this way.

Get a grip, Colin.

He strolled through the brick archway, under the faux portcullis and iron sign stating simply, "English Market." Brick floors opened to a fountain under a domed skylight with wooden trusses. Meat counters flanked the aisle. An open, second-story gallery filled with tables and chairs looked down from behind a wood and metal railing. His spring break trip to Seattle and Pike's Place Market flitted through his mind—though the Irish version was cleaner and more refined. Shop after shop lined the halls that branched off at angles, taking you deeper into the maze of stalls. The brick floor gave way to tile as Colin passed a chocolate shop and several poultry stalls. He wove through the light foot traffic, pausing to take a sample of boutique cheese made on the premises. As the salty tang spread over his taste buds, he made a note to come back and get a small block. That and a loaf of bread would do just fine for supper tonight, regardless of where he ended up.

A seafood stall boasting locally caught fish of more varieties than he'd ever seen in one place took up one entire hallway, ending in a sandwich shop on the corner. What was their definition of "local"? He paused to look at the signs and sighed. Kinsale. This whole case had been caught by fishermen in Kinsale just that morning. He'd been able to see the fishing boats from the window in the apartment above Patrick's pub and had spent many a morning sipping coffee, watching the men unload their catch. Had Rachel watched the ships come in?

Raking a hand through his hair he turned. It didn't matter. She was looking for roots and he…well, he'd tried that and been proven a failure. Let her find someone who didn't have his track record, someone who was able to be in one place without getting so unfocused that he missed all the signs of unhappiness. There had to have been signs, right? Jessica hadn't simply woken up one day and decided that, not only didn't she love him, but she no longer shared his vision for their company. Rachel deserved better than that. And even with all his failings, he deserved someone who could love and appreciate him for who he was, even if it meant he wasn't ready to find some nine-to-five job as a corporate drone. He deserved better, too.

But he wanted Rachel.

10

Rachel lowered herself to the stone wall and stared out over the bay. She'd never get tired of the view or the slight tang of salt in the wind that whipped over the cliffs, ruffling her hair. Even with tourist season moving into full swing, Kinsale managed to avoid feeling crowded. Visitors came to see Charles Fort and watch the sailboat races, and then moved on toward Blarney and the Ring of Kerry. A handful stayed the night. Siobhan was getting plenty of business, and the Pub seemed a bit fuller on the nights she joined her aunt for the evening in town. But as much as she loved it, Kinsale simply wasn't home. Why not? That was the question that plagued her.

She missed Colin. It was ridiculous. She hardly knew him, but his face lingered in her thoughts, along with his subtle humor, and the electricity that surged through her when their fingers touched. Why had he hung up so quickly last week? Should she have called him back? Calling boys—men—was something her mother had always frowned on. Rachel couldn't quite bring herself to break their unwritten rule. Besides, he'd call back if he wanted to talk to her. Right?

"Lovely view, isn't it? Can I join you?"

Rachel started, her gaze jerking up, eyes widening as they landed on Colin. "What…you're...hi." She shook her head, trying to organize her thoughts. "Sure, of course. Have a seat."

He grinned as he sat. "No work at the B&B today?"

"My aunt has things so organized and together…I'm just in the way, honestly. She tries to let me lend a hand, but anything I do takes away from the local girls she's been hiring for years to help out. Frankly, it's better to just leave things as they are. As much as it bothers me to think that the Sea Haven won't stay in our family when Siobhan passes on, it's probably for the best."

"Sorry." Colin patted her knee.

She shrugged, working to ignore the electricity shooting up her leg. Her heart was racing. Trying for a nonchalant tone, she cleared her throat. "So…what brings you back to Kinsale?"

"That's an interesting story, actually." He shifted so their eyes met. "After we spoke on the phone, I left Blarney and headed toward Cork city. None of the towns along the way had a place for me, but, no worries I thought, there had to be something in the city. Except there wasn't. I poked around for a week, playing tourist and just enjoying the town, but every day I'd end up back in the English Market at this one seafood stall, staring at the fresh catches brought in that morning from Kinsale and thinking about you."

Heat pulsed into her cheeks. The corners of her lips poked up. "Really?"

He nodded. "After a few days, the fishmonger asked me about my behavior. I guess it's a bit odd to stare at fish without ever buying something."

Rachel snickered. "Maybe a little."

"Before long, they asked me why I was still in Cork City when I needed to be back in Kinsale. And I didn't have an answer. So I checked out of my B&B, packed up the car, and your aunt said I'd probably find you down by the sea wall."

Her thoughts raced. He'd come back just because of her? "But what about…"

He laughed. "There are a lot of questions I don't have the answers to right now. But I'm hoping you'll give me—give us— the chance to find them. Together."

Was there any point? If he was determined to continue his wandering minstrel act, what possible future did they have? On the other hand…he'd come back. Because of her. That had to count for something. "I'd like that."

Tingles raced up her arm as he threaded his fingers through hers. "I'm staying in Patrick's place, above the Flat Tire. He said he'd love to have me play for as long as I wanted. Will you come hear me tonight?"

She tried not to answer too fast but the words rushed out. "Try to keep me away."

As soon as she pulled open the pub door, Rachel's gaze drifted to the corner where Colin had set up his instruments. The room was all but empty at the early hour. Even families with young children wouldn't be ready for dinner quite yet. The pub would fill up over the next two hours, especially once word got out that Colin was back. He was strumming something instrumental—she didn't recognize what—on his guitar. Electricity sizzled through her as his eyes locked on hers. How was it possible for him to have this effect on her? What was she going to do when she had to head back to the States?

With a nod to Patrick, she wove through the tables and slid into the empty booth near Colin's corner. "That's enchanting. What is it?"

"Just a tune I've been fiddling around with. I'm not sure it goes anywhere, and I've no lyrics in mind, but since the pub's still relatively empty, I thought it'd be a good time to play with it a bit more. How was your afternoon?" Colin glanced at his fingering on the neck of the guitar.

"Quiet. All the guests were out sightseeing, the ladies who do the cleaning had come and gone, and Siobhan took a nap. So…I booted up my laptop and frittered away a couple of hours trying to figure out where I should live when I go back to the States." And she'd spent entirely too long remembering their conversation on the sea wall, daydreaming about his hand in hers, and wondering what his kiss would be like. But he didn't need to know that.

Colin's eyebrows shot up. "You won't go back home?"

She lifted a shoulder. "There's nothing particularly pressing there. I mean, sure, I have a handful of school friends, but we've drifted, for the most part. So it seems like maybe the better plan is to start fresh someplace where there aren't so many memories, where Mom and Dad don't linger around every corner."

He nodded and brought the song to a close. Setting the guitar aside, he hopped down from his perch and plopped onto the bench across from her. "Any strong leanings?"

"Not really. I need to pray about it, I guess. But..." Rachel pressed her lips together. Asking meant opening herself up for him to realize how shaky her faith had become. Did she want to do that? Would he even be interested if he knew how hard she was struggling right now?

"But...?"

She sighed. "It doesn't feel like God's listening. Or if He is, He doesn't care. Or something."

Colin reached across the table to squeeze her hand. "That's hard."

Could he possibly understand? A little bit of the tightness in her chest eased. At least he hadn't come back with a quip straight off a bumper sticker or one of those cat posters. She'd had enough of those to last three lifetimes after her dad died. "Yeah, it is. And I don't know how to get past it."

"One thing that helped me was just keeping at it, even when it felt pointless. I know they say it's the definition of insanity to keep doing the same thing but expect different results, but I don't think that works with God. Keep praying, even when it feels like your prayers are bouncing off the ceiling right back onto your head. God's listening...and even more? He's working. You just might not see it yet." Colin gave her hand another squeeze as he stood. "I should get back to it. Any requests?"

She shook her head, her gaze following him back to the platform where he picked up his fiddle. As Colin coaxed a slow, mournful tune out of the strings she chewed her lip. He understood. There was no way he would've been able to describe it so perfectly if he hadn't been there. So...maybe his suggestion was worth trying. Maybe God really was listening.

11

Colin walked up the hill toward the Sea Haven B&B. Clouds
dotted the sky, promising rain later. He squinted. To his untrained
eye, it wasn't likely to be a downpour. Just more of the 'soft
weather' the Irish loved. A good day to go for a drive, maybe see
where the roads took them. If Rachel would come along, it didn't
matter if it was a dreary day. She could light up the worst storm.
He scoffed, trotting up the stairs to the front door. When had he
become a romantic sap? He pushed the buzzer.

Siobhan opened the door with a radiant smile. "And there's
himself, come to call. Come along in, Rachel's in the kitchen,
straight back. She's gotten to be a fair hand at the full Irish if
you've not yet eaten."

His stomach rumbled. He'd had a thick slice of brown bread
with butter back at the pub, but a full Irish? He'd never turn that
down. "That sounds great."

Siobhan waved him on before turning to go up the stairs.

Colin followed his nose in the direction she'd indicated. Rachel stood at the stove, an apron bearing shamrocks tied around her waist. Bacon and sausage sizzled in a cast iron skillet on one burner while she stirred eggs on another. "Morning. Your aunt said I could come on back and that maybe you'd share breakfast?"

Rachel grinned. "Can do. Some of this is for the guests—we have one couple who asked for a nine-thirty breakfast—while everyone else has already eaten and left, so there's still plenty. What are you up to today?"

"Depends." He grinned. "I was hoping I could convince you to go for a drive with me. Maybe head east and see what we find? Other than sheep, of course. We'll find plenty of those, I can already guarantee that."

Chuckling, Rachel opened the oven door and pulled out a tray of broiled tomatoes. She lifted down two plates and started arranging sausage, bacon, eggs, and black and white puddings before finishing each off with a tomato half. "That sounds fun. Though you'll have to drive—or we can see about borrowing Siobhan's car—I turned in my rental last week. It seemed to make more sense financially. And I can't say I was getting all that great at navigating the roundabouts anyway. Everyone's probably safer with me off the road."

"I can drive." Was his car clean? Or at least clean enough? Why hadn't he thought to check before he walked up to ask her to come?

"I'll be right back." Rachel took the two plates and a coffee pot through a swinging door that had to lead to the guest dining room. She was back quickly, sans plates. "Now that they're set, I'll fix ours. Do you want the pudding, too?"

Colin had enjoyed the black and white puddings when he first arrived in Ireland. Then he'd made the mistake of asking what was in them. Had it been long enough? His mouth filled with water despite the lingering memory of the main ingredients and he nodded. "Sure. Bring 'em on."

Wrinkling her nose, Rachel fixed two more plates, leaving the puddings off one. "Coffee or tea?"

"Coffee. I love tea in the afternoon, I think that's a tradition we're seriously missing out on at home. But I can't start the day without coffee."

She laughed and hooked her fingers through two mugs and a coffee pot.

"That's quite a balancing act you have there." He reached for a plate.

"I've only dropped something once. That was enough to learn my limits." Rachel filled both mugs with coffee, starting when Colin grasped her hand in his.

"Thank You, Father, for the enjoyable day you have shaping up for us today. Thank You for this incredible food and the generous and beautiful hands that prepared it. Amen."

Pink stained Rachel's cheeks as she ducked her head and began attacking her sausages with knife and fork. "Amen."

What was going through her mind? Colin gave an internal sigh, was he ever going to understand women? "Is there anywhere you've been hoping to see, now that you've set your sights on doing a little touring?"

"Cobh." Rachel took a sip of coffee to wash down the mouthful that had muddled her words. "I've been reading a little about the Lusitania, and of course everyone knows about the Titanic. It seems criminal to be this close to Cobh and not go experience that history first hand."

"All right, Cobh it is." That wasn't one of the places he'd looked up on his computer before heading up here, but it wasn't much past Cork City. Surely it wouldn't take more than a couple of hours to drive there.

"Aunt Siobhan has maps in the front room. I'll grab one after breakfast. But it's one of the places I hear her sending tourists, so it can't be too far."

"Perfect. I'll let Patrick know where we're off to, just in case we get back late. I don't think he'll mind if I miss a night—or at least part of one—but I should double check." Colin scraped the last bite together and popped it in his mouth. Aunt Siobhan had been right about Rachel's food, he'd never had a better breakfast. How much of it was the company? "Can you be ready in about thirty minutes?"

Rachel swiveled to check the clock hanging across the room and nodded. "Sure."

"Great. I'll be back, with the car." Colin carried his plate to the sink. As he passed Rachel at the small kitchen table, he leaned down and laid his cheek on her hair, his lips itching to press a kiss there. Too soon. He straightened, tossing a wink in her direction. "See you in a bit."

Patrick had been thrilled they were making the trip to Cobh. He'd sent Colin off with directions for the quickest route, skirting the southern side of Cork City, restaurant recommendations for lunch and dinner, and firm instructions not to worry about being back to play at all that evening. Colin tried to argue, but it was quickly clear that there was little point. If there was one word to describe Patrick, it'd be stubborn.

Green whizzed past the windows as they drove. There were sheep, as promised, and tiny villages that dotted the countryside.

"It's so beautiful. I keep thinking I'll get used to how lush everything is, but I just can't. Even on days like today, when the sky has that not-quite-but-almost-ominous look to it, it's just lovely." Rachel adjusted her seat, leaning back an extra notch.

"Ireland is a little slice of heaven. Though I wonder if it gets old when you're here year after year. I know I started to ignore some of the great things about Chicago when I lived there. Sure, I'd hit the beach on Lake Michigan now and again, but the museums and the restaurants…most of the time I was too busy to bother. Life gets in the way, you know?"

Rachel nodded. "It's a little different when you're in the tourism business. You have to keep your finger on the pulse somewhat, but yeah...we definitely got too busy to enjoy the mountains when we were neck deep in rentals. Still...it's disappointing that I won't have the chance to see if that happens in Ireland as easily as it does in the States. I guess I envy you a little."

Colin pursed his lips. Did she think he was living here permanently? Sure, he didn't have any definite plans to head back to the US, but it wasn't as if he'd planned to live here indefinitely either. He had to go back at some point. "I'm not..."

"Let's not talk about it, okay? Look." Rachel pointed to the glistening water out the window.

12

Rachel stretched and looked out over the railing that separated the water from the sidewalk. Colin was still taking photos of the statue of Annie Moore and her two brothers, the first emigrant to be processed at Ellis Island. She'd read about them on the drive over—maybe someday she'd get to New York City and see the matching statue there. New York...could she...no. Sure, there were probably plenty of opportunities for jobs in hospitality there, but she wasn't a city girl.

"Ready?" Colin tucked his camera in his pocket. "The Queenstown Story here at the Heritage Center is supposed to be fantastic. Or we could hop on one of the boat tours and see the harbor, hear the recorded spiel about the Lusitania and the Titanic."

"I'm not ready to sit again yet."

He laughed. "The museum it is."

They crossed the parking lot where they'd left the car and bought tickets to the Heritage Center. They wandered through the quiet rooms of the restored Victorian train station, looking at exhibits detailing the potato famine and the vast emigration of Irish to America. From there, they read about the rescue of the Lusitania survivors and the heroic efforts of the local fishermen on behalf of those souls, as well as the notoriety the town gained as the last stop before the Titanic met its end. The town had a somber history, though the museum had taken care to highlight as many happy stories as they could.

Toward the end of the tour, Colin slipped his fingers through hers. "Do you want to grab a bite to eat in the café here, or find one of the restaurants Patrick suggested?"

"I'm actually not all that hungry yet. Do you think we could find one of those harbor tours now, maybe eat afterward?"

He grinned. "Sure. Let's ask at the desk, I'm sure they can point us in the right direction."

The harbor tour, complete with tea and sandwiches, had given them a taste of the history and daily life in Cobh. It was a bustling small town, proud of its ancestry and fiercely connected to life on the water. What must it be like to have such strong roots? Rachel sighed. She wanted that. Could you find it, though, if you weren't born into it?

They strolled through the park along the water's edge before crossing the road to view the Lusitania memorial up close. Surrounded by brightly colored buildings, an angel stood above two men, one with his head bowed, the other looking up to the sky. Tears pooled in her eyes. Why was the simplicity of the statue so moving?

Colin slipped his arm around her shoulders and snugged her to his side. After several minutes, his cell phone chirped.

"Do you need to get that?"

He shook his head. "It's just another email from Jessica. She's not getting the hint."

Jessica? Wasn't that his ex? Rachel wiggled out from his embrace and frowned. "What hint would that be?"

He reached for her hand, his eyebrows drawing together when she tucked her hands in her pockets. "That I'm not interested in coming back to the company to be part of her little dog and pony show. Let's walk and I'll fill you in."

All the warmth evaporated from the day. Why had she thought she knew him? Hadn't her parents always warned her that physical attraction was the worst possible way to start a relationship? And yet, here she was, half in love with someone she'd just met, all because of the current that jolted through her when their fingers met.

"I tried to tell you about this in the car. You know the basics—Jessica went behind my back and made a deal to sell the company. She thought I'd go along with it, even though she knew I'd be initially upset, I think she felt like the fact that we were dating gave her an edge. But in reality, that just made it worse. Had we not been involved I might have been less upset. The deal…it wasn't terrible. But it wasn't something we needed. And I wanted to make it on our own, not because we got some fancy board and venture capital." He stopped and nodded to a tea shop with outdoor tables. "Want to sit for a bit, have some tea?"

Rachel shrugged. What she wanted to do was get in the car and go back to Kinsale, pack her bags, and go back to…somewhere Colin wasn't. There had to be some way to escape this mortification, didn't there? Who kept in contact with their ex if there was nothing still between them? Maybe it was possible…just not particularly probable, and she wasn't interested in being a rebound girlfriend. Even if he wasn't painting her in a great light...why risk it? *Been there, done that.* Unfortunately, he was her ride so she might as well have some tea and hear him out. Maybe, just maybe, he'd convince her that she wasn't a fool of the highest order.

A cheery bell jingled as Colin pushed open the door and held it for her. Counter height tables and stools lined the far wall; a gleaming display case full of glistening pastries ran down the near wall. A young woman looked up from a book and smiled. "Can I help you?"

Colin glanced at Rachel and arched a brow.

She eyed the chalkboard behind the counter. She hadn't had an actual cream tea yet. It sounded like just the thing. "I'd like the cream tea, please."

"Make it two. That sounds perfect. Can we sit outside?"

The young woman nodded. "Sure. I'll bring it right out."

Rachel reached for her purse as the cash register beeped.

Colin set his hand on her arm. "Let me. Please?"

"All right. Thanks." Rachel fought the heat that spread through her from his touch. He was a gentleman...which meant he probably wasn't getting back together with Jessica. Or maybe he was and that's why he hadn't kissed her when they were sitting on the sea wall. But if he was, then why had he come back to Kinsale? She bit back a sigh, her heart softening. If he was worth potentially giving up her dream of a stable, rooted home, he was worth hearing out. No one ever got far jumping to conclusions.

When they were seated beneath a green and white striped umbrella, a steaming pot of tea and array of cream-filled pastries and scones between them, Colin continued.

"Where was I? The deal. Well, I cashed out rather than be made a figurehead in the company I built from the ground up. Maybe it wasn't the most mature move—plenty of people accused me of throwing a hissy fit—but it felt right. Honestly, it still feels right. It brought me to Ireland where, apart from seeing this incredible country and getting a chance to experience life as a traveling musician, I met you."

Rachel looked down and stirred her tea.

The slightest frown passed over his face before he bit into a scone slathered in clotted cream. He washed the bite down with tea and dug out his phone, dropping it on the table. "In Blarney, I started getting emails from Jessica. The board wants me to come back, head up a Federal services arm of the company in the DC area. Reading between the lines, I'd say they've hit a bit of a financial bump and are hoping to bolster their bottom line with the somewhat more stable prospect of government contracting. If they can win enough business that way, they'll have enough to funnel into research and development for the corporate product that's our—their—specialty and keep everything in the black. But they've got to be desperate to reach out to me. Jessica knows how I feel about Federal contracts."

"What's wrong with them?" Rachel furrowed her brow. Even though she'd grown up near the West Virginia border, there were plenty of people who made the trek into DC every day. Government contracting jobs kept afloat plenty of people she knew.

"Nothing, really. But it's not anything I ever wanted to get into. Primarily because it's just not a good fit for the kinds of products and services we were focused on." Colin shrugged. "Jessica was always pushing in the direction. Why she's not heading up the Federal arm is beyond me."

"Have you asked her?"

He shook his head. "I haven't responded to any of the emails. I was hoping that she'd get the hint. I cashed out. Sure, it's nice that they're willing to hire me back, but if I'm going to simply be an employee, it's going to be in a company I didn't help found."

That made sense. Rachel picked at a currant in her scone, flicking it until it popped out of the treat and onto her plate. Why did people ruin perfectly good baked goods with dried fruit? "So you're not going to DC?"

"I don't even know. I can stay in Ireland a few more months before I have to make a decision about what's next. And there's a whole world out there, you know?"

Her heart sank as she nodded. He had no plans to settle. She'd known that. Why had she hoped that might change? Even if he'd wanted to settle somewhere in the States and flit around semi-locally, they might have been able to make things work. But if he was going to move from country to country and see the world? Well, even if she could afford to do it, she craved a place to call home. You couldn't find that living out of a suitcase. She pushed the thoughts away and drained her tea.

"That hit the spot. Want to walk around a bit and see the rest of the town before we head back? I thought I might try and find a thank you gift for my aunt."

Colin gave her a long look before standing. "Sure. Let's see what we can find."

13

Colin watched Rachel from the corner of his eye as he navigated the increasingly narrow roads that led into Kinsale. Something was wrong, though he couldn't quite nail down what. She'd been chatty as they walked the hilly streets of Cobh, poking in every boutique they ran across. But she hadn't said anything important.

He pulled his car into an empty space in the Sea Haven's small lot. Rachel had the door open before he'd turned off the engine.

"Rachel, wait."

She turned, one leg already out of the car. "Yeah?"

"Let me walk you to the door." He wanted to ask what was wrong, but all the combinations he tried in his head sounded needy and pathetic.

"It's just right there." She pointed to the well-lit door not twenty feet away.

"I know that…I just…please?" He pushed open his door and hurried around the car. At least she hadn't made a run for the B&B. "Can I carry your bag?"

Eyebrows lifting, Rachel gave him the small paper bag containing a stained-glass window-hanging handcrafted by a local Cobh artist.

Colin shut the passenger door and walked with Rachel toward the house. "Thanks for coming out with me today."

She stopped and turned toward him, one half of her mouth quirked into a smile. "I had fun. And I can cross Cobh off my list now, which means I hit all of the major sites in County Cork that were on my must-see list. So thank you."

"Rachel…" He slipped his arm around her waist and pulled her toward himself, his lips descending to hers. She stiffened for a moment, then stepped closer, her hand slipping around his head, her fingers threading through his hair. Lightning arced through him and his hand curled to a fist in the small of her back. Struggling against himself, he eased back, unable to stop a smile when she tried to follow.

"Wow." Rachel took a quick, deep breath, her eyes meeting his. Her neck and cheeks were flushed, her eyes glassy. She pressed her lips together. "Um. Okay then."

He followed as she turned and walked to the front door. "Did you want your aunt's gift?"

She blinked and took the bag from him. "Right. Thanks."

"See you tomorrow?"

Rachel nodded.

Smiling, Colin lowered his head for a final, soft kiss. "'Night, then."

"Right. 'Night." Confusion spread over her features as she looked down at the doorknob.

Colin reached around her and turned the handle, pushing the door open. She flashed him a semi-dazed smile as she went in. He pulled the door closed and tucked his hands in his pockets, whistling merrily as he went back to his car.

Patrick was already busily chopping vegetables when Colin made his way down from the apartment above the pub. All the fresh air and walking, not to mention too many hours puzzling over Rachel after he should have been sleeping, had made for a later start than he expected.

"'Morning." Colin shuffled toward the coffee machine in the corner of the kitchen.

"That it is. A good one, to boot." Patrick's knife paused as he looked up to grin. "How'd you enjoy Cobh?"

Colin carried his coffee to the end of the counter, out of the way of the food prep, and boosted himself up. "It was great. The Heritage Center's done a great job of making the history come alive and the harbor tour did the rest. Seeing the town was nice too, though it's not Kinsale."

"Ha. That it's not, but no place is. You like it here, then?" Patrick scooped the finely diced vegetables into a tall stock pot.

"I do." Colin blew across the rim of his mug.

Patrick pulled two whole chickens from the fridge and began running them under the water in the sink. "And Rachel?"

"She seemed to enjoy the town as well." Colin sipped.

Patrick shot him a look and transferred the chickens to a large cutting board. He began to separate the birds into pieces, neatly removing the bones. "That's not what I meant."

Colin sighed. His lips tingled when he remembered their kiss, but what about all that happened before? "I know...but I don't think I understand women. I thought we were having a good time. Then I got an email from someone back home who's trying to get me to come back and start up a new arm of the company and the next thing I know, Rachel's shifted from friendly to painfully polite."

"Hmm. And you've no idea what you said?"

"Nope."

With deft movements, Patrick diced the raw chicken and tossed it into the same stock pot as the vegetables. "She's more like her aunt than she realizes. So what will you do?"

Shrugging, Colin lifted the mug to his lips. The kisses had to mean something, didn't they? "Wait and see, I guess. I'm not in a hurry to go anywhere."

"Just don't wait too long, or you'll end up with a lifetime of regret." Patrick's shoulders slumped and he managed a sad smile.

Colin slid off the counter and drained his mug before setting in the dish sink. "Your life's not over yet, why don't you do something to change the regret?"

Patrick's hand paused reaching for a large container of what looked like homemade chicken stock. He shook his head but said nothing.

Colin opened his mouth then snapped it shut. What was there to say? It wasn't as if he had a fantastic track record in the romance department, but it made his heart ache to see two people so clearly in love live for so long without one another. He climbed the stairs to the apartment. Time to figure out a plan and put it in action.

14

Rachel rinsed the last of the breakfast dishes and set them in the drying rack next to the sink. Aunt Siobhan was busy checking out the last of the guests and sending them on their way. The two women who did the cleaning would be here before long turning the rooms, though there were no guests on the books for tonight yet. She poured another cup of coffee and sat at the kitchen table.

What was she supposed to do? That kiss…heat crept across her cheeks. Even the gentler, more perfunctory good night kiss had been…incredible. And yet…how did you fall in love with someone who might not be over their ex and was content to live from one day to the next with no purpose or plan? It wasn't that she couldn't appreciate adventure—that was a large part of why she'd come to Ireland in the first place—but even adventure needed some boundaries. She could have stayed in the States and struck out on her own, but she'd thought—hoped—that the Sea Haven would need her as much as she needed it. Now, well, maybe it was time to admit that she didn't belong and go back, find her home.

Aunt Siobhan bustled into the kitchen and sat with a sigh. "Ah now, they're off and we're free for a bit, 'til the phone rings with a booking. Will you and your young man go out touring again today?"

Rachel shook her head. "I don't think so. I haven't heard from Colin and, well, I think maybe it's time I thought about going back. You don't need me here, and I want to be somewhere I'm useful."

Siobhan pursed her lips. "Are you sure? I love having you here. Even though you think you're not useful, you're company, and you can't put a price on that at my age."

"Thanks, Aunt Siobhan. It may be a few more days. I need to figure out where I'm going, what I'll do, but I think it's time I stopped running. It's what Mom and Dad would both want."

Her aunt's list in hand, Rachel skipped down the steps from the back entrance of the B&B and headed into town. She'd miss doing the shopping at little stores that specialized in one or two things. Sausage and puddings from the butcher, bread from the bakery. She'd pop into the supermarket for a few items, but mostly she frequented little mom and pop businesses run by people who took the time to chat and get to know their customers.

A little brass bell jangled when she pushed open the bakery door. Sarah, the baker's daughter, smiled from behind the display case.

"Morning, Rachel. What's on your aunt's list today?"

Rachel grinned and consulted the paper. "She's making some soda bread today, but she needs two loaves of brown bread and something sweet for after dinner tonight. She wasn't specific on that score."

"Take a look and see what you think will fit the bill, I'll bag up the brown bread for you."

She scanned the offerings. What would her aunt like? Rachel pointed to a small cake covered in glistening chocolate. "What's that?"

"Oh, that's a little slice of heaven. It's like an éclair, but with cake instead of pastry. Wait, I think I have a slice in the back that we're going to put out as samples later. Let me see." She disappeared into the back room, returning shortly with a cupcake wrapper holding a small square of cake speared with a toothpick.

Rachel popped the bite in her mouth. "Mmm. That. I'll take that. This is sinful."

The young woman laughed and slipped the cake out of the case into a box. "'Tis. Can I get you anything else?"

"That should do it. Thanks." Rachel dug in her pocket for the Euro coins to pay the bill. Even after several weeks, using primarily coins threw her for a loop. She gave a cheery wave as she exited the shop, turning left and continuing on her way toward the butcher. It was a gorgeous day. The sky was a deep blue, unmarked by clouds, and the breeze off the water stirred the air just enough that there was no chance of getting too hot. Perfect. She paused and watched the boats racing, their colorful sails a contrast to the gleaming white of their hulls. If she could just find a place like this—a small, friendly town on the water—in the States. There had to be some, it was simply a matter of finding one that needed a B&B.

Where had that thought come from? She'd planned to find work in a hotel, maybe a smaller inn, sure, but opening her own business wasn't something she'd considered. Could she? She had the skills, that wasn't an issue. The money…well, there'd been a tiny bit left over after she'd sold the cabins and paid off all the bills. She wouldn't own anything free and clear but it might just be enough to convince a bank that she deserved a loan.

By the time Rachel made it back to the Sea Haven with her aunt's shopping complete, she had the beginnings of a plan. She breezed into the living room and stopped. Her aunt and Patrick sat embracing on the sofa.

"Sorry. I…should I have come in the back? I'll just go through to the kitchen."

"No dear, it's fine." Siobhan eased away from Patrick, though their fingers remained intertwined. "In fact, 'tis good that you're the first to know. Patrick and I are going to be married."

Married? At their age? Rachel battled the bubble of laughter that formed in her chest. "Congratulations. That's wonderful."

"Oh, I know it seems silly. But even after all this time, he's the one for me. Always has been. And now, with nothing and no one to stand in our way, we're going to make the most of what time we have left and spend it together." Siobhan's head dropped to Patrick's shoulder. He beamed down at her.

"I'm happy for you. I hope I'll be able to come back over for the wedding. I'd like to be here."

"Actually, we were planning to do something small and simple as soon as we can get the forms processed. Neither of us wants a big to-do at this point. We'll speak to the minister this afternoon, but I'm thinking it'll be this weekend at the latest. You'll stand up for me, won't you?"

"Of course, Aunt Siobhan." Rachel crossed the room and gave each of them a tight hug. "I'll let you get back to planning and go put these groceries away."

Back in her room, Rachel closed the door and allowed herself a chuckle. Marrying Patrick after all this time…well, why not? They'd certainly waited long enough. She flipped open her laptop and waited while it connected to the B&B's Wi-Fi. She'd stay until after the wedding, then head back and get started on making her own home. Her stomach twisted. It meant giving up on learning more about Colin, getting to know him better, maybe more of those bone-melting kisses. But if they had no future, then, well, it was for the best.

Rachel opened a search engine and began to poke around. She found several listings that had potential, but she kept coming back to one in Annapolis, Maryland. She'd visited Annapolis numerous times during her childhood, though she hadn't been recently. Still, what she did remember was a friendly small town on the water. And with the Naval Academy there…well, there'd always be plenty of visitors looking for a place to spend the night. Throw in the near proximity to D.C., with all the tourism that brought, and it might be the perfect location for someone wanting to run a year-round inn. She sent a quick email to the listing agent and another to her bank. She might not be able to make all the arrangements from Ireland, but she could get the balls rolling.

15

The week was a blur of wedding preparations. While Siobhan and Patrick were having a simple church ceremony, they'd both lived in Kinsale their entire lives and there were plenty of people who were excited about joining in their celebration. The handful of bookings were easily rescheduled or moved to another local B&B if the dates to be in the area were firm. With that handled, Siobhan closed the B&B. Without guests to worry about, she hounded Rachel with details. They took a day in Cork City for shopping, returning with new dresses and a trousseau for her aunt. It was sweet, really, that her aunt was going to so much trouble.

Rachel had bumped into Colin around Kinsale a few times as well. Patrick appeared to be keeping him busy with errands as well. Since so many of the locals relied on The Flat Tire for their evening gatherings, Patrick couldn't close completely. Colin had, apparently, offered to help out. Every time she spotted him, Rachel's lips began to tingle. Would he kiss her again? But he never seemed tempted. He'd hinted that maybe they should stop and grab a bite, or some tea, but she'd always been on the way to something that couldn't wait. Besides, she was leaving and he'd be off on another adventure. A future with Colin could never be more than a pleasant daydream.

Now, she was standing in the back of an old stone church wearing a moss green chiffon dress that floated down from an empire waist to just below her knees. Her aunt, in a simple ivory silk suit, complete with a pillbox hat that had a small net veil, clasped and unclasped her hands as the organ played.

"Take a deep breath, Aunt Siobhan." Rachel pulled her aunt into a tight hug. "Our cue's coming."

"It's ridiculous to be nervous at my age, but I am. Have I jumped into this too quickly?" Siobhan twisted a handkerchief in her gloved hands.

Rachel shook her head. Rushed? They'd been effectively courting for the last fifty-some years. This was well overdue. "Aunt Siobhan, why would you wait any longer? You've loved Patrick since you were young, and he's loved you that same time. If anything, you should have jumped into this sooner."

Her aunt ran her hands down her skirt, smoothing the fabric. She let out a breath. "Thank you, dear…you don't think it's dumb then, us marrying when we're so old?"

"No. I think it's charming and right. And I'm happy to be here to see it happen. The two of you are going to have some wonderful years together. I just wish things had worked out for you before now."

The organ swelled to a crescendo and the church's wedding coordinator pulled open the doors that led to the sanctuary, cutting off her aunt's reply.

"Here we go." Rachel kissed Siobhan's cheek and started her slow walk down the aisle. Patrick stood at the altar, palpable anticipation pulsing off him. Next to him was...Colin? She missed her footing, tweaking her ankle, and fought for balance. She wasn't going to fall on her face in front of everyone. She just wasn't. A few more out of synch steps had her back in tempo with the music. What was Colin doing as best man? Surely Patrick had a friend, nephew, someone—anyone—else who was a better choice? And why hadn't Siobhan said something?

Rachel reached the front of the church and took her place, turning as the music changed to *Sheep May Safely Graze*. Her aunt stepped through the doors and paused. Rachel watched as Siobhan scanned the crowd before her gaze connected with Patrick's. A smile bloomed on her face and she strode down the aisle a little faster than the music called for, all traces of her previous nervousness gone. The organist brought the music to a close and the minister began the ceremony.

"Quite a sight, wasn't it?" Colin bumped Rachel's shoulder with his as he took one of the stools along the bar in Patrick's pub.

"It was beautiful. It's nice to think that love can last for so long under such difficult circumstances. Though I'm sad for the years that were wasted. They're so perfect for one another." Rachel frowned into her sparkling water before taking a drink. "And I wish my dad had been here. He always loved his older sister…he would've been thrilled for her."

Colin reached over and squeezed her hand. "Sorry." His mumble was barely audible over the cheering of the crowd in the pub.

"No, it's all right." Rachel swiveled and nodded toward the platform where a group of seven musicians were wedged. "Why aren't you up there?"

He grinned. "I offered. Turns out I'm not the only talented musician in Kinsale. Who knew?"

She laughed. "Well, it's nice you get a night off."

"It'll be nicer if you'll let me spend some of it with you."

Her heart leapt, but she quickly squelched the bubble of joy. Was there a point? She was leaving. He was staying—or continuing to roam—neither of which amounted to the two of them ending up together. And yet…she hadn't left yet, and this would be one more set of memories to cherish in the years ahead. "I'd like that."

Colin looked over his shoulder. "C'mon, let's dance."

Rachel followed his glance. The tables had been moved out of the way and couples were whirling about in some sort of fast-paced dance. "No way."

"What?" He turned in his seat so he faced the dance floor, head cocked to one side. "We could totally do that."

Rachel snickered. "Not without knocking over everyone who's already out there."

"It can't be that hard." Colin waved to the bartender. "What's this dance called?"

"Haymaker's Jig, you ought to know, you've played the music for it often enough."

Colin shrugged. "I recognized the tune, didn't know it was the dance, too. Is it hard to learn?"

The bartender laughed. "Depends on how coordinated you are."

Rachel watched the man move back down the length of the bar and lifted her hands in front of her chest. "Uh-uh. If it's relying on coordination, I'm out. Your feet would never be the same."

Colin narrowed his eyes. "Fine. We'll wait for something slower, but I *will* get you out on that dance floor. It's your aunt's wedding, you have to dance a little."

"We'll see." She nodded to where Siobhan and Patrick were kicking up their heels in quick steps. "I don't honestly think she'll notice one way or the other."

Colin slid his arm along the bar behind her, his hand curling around her shoulder. "Are they planning a honeymoon?"

She wiggled back on her stool so his arm touched across her back, its comforting warmth seeping through her dress. "They'll stay at his mother's house tonight, then move to the B&B for a week. Siobhan cancelled the bookings, after making sure that the inn down the street could take them. No one seemed to mind."

His eyebrow winged up. "Wouldn't it be less crowded at his mother's house?"

Rachel took a deep breath as her stomach twisted. This was the conversation she'd been dreading. Of course it was too much to ask to just be able to avoid it. "I'm leaving in the morning."

16

"Leaving?" She couldn't be leaving…he was just getting ready to put his plan into play. If he'd known she was going away he wouldn't have been so casual about his attempts to spend time with her during the past week. He hadn't been avoiding her—not completely—but he'd wanted to keep her wondering. Had it worked too well?

"I found a place in Annapolis that's for sale. It's…a little pricey, but with the little bit I have left from my parent's estate, the bank seems confident they can get me a business loan for the rest. It's had good, steady business the past five years. The owners are just looking to retire. It's too much of an answer to prayer to not jump on."

"What do you mean answer to prayer?" Colin clenched his hand into a fist. Patrick and Siobhan's wedding was an answer to *his* prayer, one that would help Rachel see that love was worth waiting for, even in the face of seemingly insurmountable obstacles.

"I can't stay here. I thought coming to Ireland was a new adventure, a way to get a clean slate and start fresh. When I realized Siobhan didn't need me…well, I had to face the fact that I was just running away. That was sobering. I wasn't raised to run when it got hard—so I'm going back and I'm going to make it work. It's not the Shenandoah, but it's the same region. That's one part of Ireland I *am* taking with me—Annapolis is a small town on the water. I'm going to make it into the home I'd hoped Kinsale would be."

Colin puffed out his cheeks, blowing out a breath. It was hard to argue with that logic. But what about his prayers? Rachel mattered. A lot. For the first time in…a while…Colin could actually picture a future with someone. Even when he and Jessica had been at their strongest, the future was a nebulous blur. "Do you have to go so fast? I was hoping, now that all the wedding errands are taken care of, we could do some more exploring together."

Rachel frowned. "Sorry. I already changed my ticket…and Siobhan and Patrick are planning on holing up in the B&B. I guess his childhood home wasn't really high on either of their lists for a honeymoon. Plus, I don't want to lose this inn and I can't help feeling that negotiations are going to be easier with me there in the same time zone."

"Yeah. Of course they are." He scrubbed a hand over his face and swallowed the lump in his throat. It landed as a lead ball in his stomach. She was leaving just like that, which left him…where? *Deal with that later. Don't waste your last night with her.* He forced his mouth into a smile. "Then you definitely owe me a dance since I won't be able to collect later."

A sliver of moon shone down through the clouds as Colin slipped his fingers through Rachel's. The reception was breaking up. Siobhan and Patrick had said their goodbyes about a half an hour previously and the rest of the crowd had followed shortly after. Now he and Rachel were slowly climbing the hill to the Sea Haven. It was the last time he'd make the trip. Since she had to get to the airport early the next morning, Rachel had arranged for a taxi. Without her to hold him to Kinsale, Colin was going to move on tomorrow as well. Maybe it was time to move north. Someplace where there weren't cliffs and beaches to bring her to mind.

"Are you sure you have to go?" The lead in his stomach grew heavier each time he asked, but he couldn't stop the words.

"I am." Rachel stopped and turned, locking her gaze with his. "I'm sorry."

He lowered his forehead to hers. "Me too."

Cheeks aching from the effort, Colin forced another smile and resumed walking. They reached the steps to the inn much too quickly.

Rachel paused, her hand on the knob. "Maybe when you come back to the US you'll look me up?"

"Rachel…" Could she hear his heart breaking?

She stood on her toes and pressed her lips to his. She probably meant it to be friendly, but it touched off a storm. He pulled her into his arms, crushing his lips against hers, willing her to understand how much he needed her not to leave.

Slowly, Rachel eased back with a wistful smile. She pushed open the door and pressed a finger to his lips. He clamped down on the words that threatened to spill out. He wasn't going to beg again. At some point, he had to salvage his pride, didn't he? Eyes burning, he watched as she stepped inside and closed the door. The finality of the lock's click pierced what was left of his heart.

Colin shoved his hands in his pockets. How had such a promising day turned out so poorly? He'd been sure that their relationship was on the right path—that she'd understood his explanation of why he'd returned to Kinsale. Had he been wrong? Didn't she realize he was in love with her? He kicked a pebble, sending it skittering into the street.

Restless, he looked down the lane to the pub. He should go back and help tidy up. It was the least he could do with all Patrick had done for him. He turned the other direction and headed toward the water. He'd help later. For now…he needed to think.

17

Rachel stood outside the Federal-style brick home. It was narrower than she'd expected, almost like a town home, though it was detached, barely, from the more Victorian looking home next door. Porches on each of the three stories ran the full length of one of the longer sides of the building, each holding several rocking chairs and…were those glass tables? Guests could eat outside, perhaps, on nice mornings. Traffic on the street was light, despite it being the middle of rush hour. She could just catch the glint of sun off the water at the end of the street.

"Sorry I'm late." An older woman in a power suit closed the door of her SUV and strode to the sidewalk. The car beeped and its lights flashed as she extended her hand to Rachel. "I'm Carla with Annapolis Realty. You're Rachel?"

"That's me. It's nice to meet you in person, though I appreciate how much you've been willing to do through emails."

"My pleasure. Let's go on in. There aren't any guests right now, so the owners said we could have a full tour."

Rachel slipped a notepad out of her purse as they climbed the stairs to the front porch. There were a few shutters that needed to be repainted, or possibly replaced, as well as two loose bricks on the main path. She noted them down. Hopefully there weren't going to be considerable repairs needed inside, though it might help drive the price down, and that wasn't a terrible thing to consider.

Carla held open the front door. Rachel let out a breath. Gleaming wood floors led down a narrow hall. Elegant wallpaper evoked the spirit of the Federal era with its dark blue background, cream flowers, and colorful birds that drew the eye up the staircase on the right.

"As you can see, the entryway is elegant, though smaller in keeping with the original footprint of the home."

"The floors are original?" Rachel squatted to run her hand over the planks.

"Yes. Though they've been very well maintained throughout. I believe any of the furnishings you see are also available for purchase and the window coverings are included at no additional charge."

That was nice. The hall stand, with its marble top and ornate carving was a beautiful piece that set the tone nicely. How much were they asking for that? Maybe they'd make her a deal if she took the whole place as is—it would certainly save some time getting open if she bought the place completely furnished.

Carla led the way through two parlors off the main hall and back into the kitchen. "This area has been completely modernized and is set up for commercial cooking."

Rachel ran a hand over the marble countertops and stepped closer to the stainless steel six burner range. "Gas cooking?"

Carla consulted her listing sheet. "Yes. And gas heat."

The butler's pantry opened into the guest dining room, set with several tables for four guests each. A picture window looked out over a shaded brick patio with white iron tables and chairs. An alcove led to a back staircase to the main guest floor. Each of the four guest rooms had its own en suite bath and a generous king-sized bed. The rooms on the front of the house had doors leading to a shared balcony overlooking a grassy park. Rooms in the back viewed the patio from their windows. The back staircase continued to the third floor, which the current owners had turned into their own space with two bedrooms with en suites, a kitchenette, and a small family room.

"Separate owner's area. But you're never too far from your guests."

Rachel pursed her lips. "But no door to keep guests from wandering up."

"It would be easy enough to put a door at the bottom of the stairs to keep this separate." Carla offered a bright smile. "Do you have any questions?"

"Have you got any sense about how firm they are on their selling price?" There were a number of things Rachel would need to freshen, though the majority of the inn was in great shape, blending Federal era décor with modern conveniences. Still, she'd want to add her personal touch to make it her own, especially up here where she'd be living. Though that could wait until she had some revenue coming in, if it had to.

"It's been on the market a while, so there's probably at least a little wiggle room. You can always make an offer and see what happens."

Rachel pulled her lip between her teeth. Was she going to do this? Butterflies danced in her stomach, but that was natural, wasn't it? Buying property was a big undertaking, but if she pushed aside the nerves…there was peace. This was right. "Let's put an offer together."

By the end of the week, the contract was signed and everything was moving rapidly toward closing. The owners had graciously allowed Rachel to move into one of the guest rooms while they packed their personal belongings from the third floor. She'd purchased the rest of the furniture with the B&B. Even if she ended up redecorating, she could sell what she didn't keep for more than she'd paid. Since the couple who'd previously owned the inn was moving onto their boat and planning to spend their retirement sailing the world, they were shedding as many of their possessions as possible.

Rachel poked her head into the kitchen. "That smells fantastic. Can I help with anything?"

George, with his navy and white striped chef's apron tied over khakis and a pink polo, shook his head. "I've got it. I might actually miss this part of inn keeping. Making people breakfast every morning, getting a chance to see the town through their eyes, not to mention built-in guinea pigs for new recipes...those have been the highlights of our time here."

Rachel slid onto a stool at the island. "And the lowlights?"

"Scrubbing five bathrooms every day and the mountains of laundry."

She chuckled. Those had been the worst parts of the cabin rentals as well, though they'd only had turn over once a week. Still, she could handle it.

"Why don't you go have a seat with the other guests? Then, when breakfast is over, I'll let you help me freshen the rooms."

"Deal." Rachel paused on the threshold of the kitchen. "Thanks, George. You and Silvia have been so helpful with this transition. I'm going to miss you."

Once breakfast was over, Rachel waved goodbye to the guests. She turned to see George and Silvia, suitcases at their feet, standing in the foyer.

"I guess this is it." Silvia turned and looked lovingly down the hall then back at Rachel. "I know you'll take good care of her. And if you need anything we've left you our email address. I wish we'd have more reliable phone connections…"

"I'll be fine. I appreciate all you've done for me. Now you two go and sail the seas—send me a photo now and then though, okay?"

Silvia pulled Rachel into a tight hug. "Of course. And you send us pictures of what you change. I know you'll make the Egret even lovelier and I can't wait to see how you personalize the place."

Rachel extended a hand to George. He rolled his eyes and wrapped her in a bear hug. "Handshakes are for strangers, you're the daughter we always wished we could have. You be good to the old gal and she'll do right by you. And try to find yourself a young man…lovely girl like you shouldn't be alone for the rest of her life."

Murmuring a response, tears filled her eyes. She blinked them back and swallowed, hoping to ease the ache in her chest. She raised a hand in farewell as George and Silvia carted their bags out to the waiting taxi. Would she be alone if she'd stayed in Ireland? Would Colin have changed his mind? Found a reason to settle down? She'd been gone three weeks now, and there'd been only a few breezy emails with photos of this or that from his journeys in Donegal. The last she'd heard from him—four days ago—he'd been planning to sail to France and see what the Continent had to offer. No. To Colin, adventure meant traveling.

She closed the door and turned, surveying the foyer—*her* foyer. Her adventure was here.

18

Colin reclined his seat and stretched his legs out under the seat in front of him. The reserved seating lounge on the ferry from Dublin to Cherbourg, France was relatively empty. Most people probably wanted a cabin for the nineteen hour cruise. Plus the ship just wasn't that crowded. He could have brought his car, but he wasn't sure about a left-hand drive when the roads switched back to right hand lanes. It could be done—postal workers all managed fine—but the added challenge when he didn't speak a lick of French seemed silly. He couldn't take it back to the States anyway. Not that he was going back anytime soon, but it never hurt to be able to go where you wanted when the whim struck. A car just slowed down that process.

He connected his cell phone to the ship's wireless Internet with a smile. All the luxuries of home. Three more email messages from Jessica. She was getting desperate. What was going on? A week ago he'd broken down and called one of the coworkers he still chatted with occasionally. Mark hadn't been able to talk long but the little Colin could glean was that Jessica's position as CEO was on the line if she didn't get Colin back. He snorted. Served her right. He felt a tiny twinge of guilt…what would her leaving mean to the company? None of the original founders would be left. Did he owe them anything? He hit reply.

Jessica,

I'd hoped you'd take a hint and stop wasting your time and mine. I'm not interested. Go find someone gullible enough to believe anything you say. At this point, I don't trust you to give me the proper time of day if we're both looking at the same clock.

-C

He re-read the message. Maybe there was still a little unresolved bitterness. He prayed constantly that God would help him forgive her. It was still a more pleasant email than any he'd composed in his head before he met Rachel. His chest tightened and the familiar ache seeped through him. He'd tried keeping in touch with Rachel via email a few times, but it was too hard. She'd gone ahead and bought the B&B and it looked and sounded incredible. But…did she miss him at all?

His phone chimed with an incoming message from Jessica. He scanned it and blew out a breath. Fine. He punched in her number and waited.

"Oh, Colin, thank God." Jessica's voice had lost all the calm assurance he'd always associated with her. Instead, panic skimmed its edges.

"This is just a phone call, Jess. Not an agreement of any sort. I need you to be perfectly clear on that or I'm hanging up."

"Okay, fine. Just hear me out. Please?"

"Start talking." Colin leaned forward and rested his elbows on his knees.

"First…I'm sorry. I know it doesn't mean anything at this point, but I was wrong to go behind your back with the sale. And…now that I know how it feels to be on the receiving end of that kind of treatment, well, I understand why you left. Regardless of that, we now have contracts in the pipeline and no office to deal with them. We're just not set up to handle the additional business—or the technology required for completion—but the board was adamant that we need the contracts. I don't know whose idea it was, though I'm trying to figure that out."

"How do you not know? You're the CEO. What were you doing? Sleeping?"

Her sigh created static on the line. "I'm not proud of it, okay. But I need help now, or I'm going to be out and then everything you worked to build…it's done. They'll shut down the commercial end of the company and become just another government contracting shop."

"It's a little late to play that card, Jess. I sold my interest in the company. Everything I worked to build? It's not mine anymore. Why don't you find a sub-contractor? Get them to do the government stuff."

"I tried suggesting that. They want you—they seem convinced that this'll get you back. Honestly, I think it's less about the contracts than an attempt to lure you back on board. Will you at least talk to them, please?"

He didn't want to talk to them. There wasn't anything they could say that would convince him to come back—especially not for government work. But if the meeting was in D.C…he could see Rachel. Maybe…a plan began to take shape. Maybe this was the second—third?—chance he needed. "Tell you what. You get me a ticket from Paris to D.C. and I'll talk to them. But I don't want you there. I'm not going to say yes, but if I tell them 'no' to their face, maybe that'll get them off your back. After this, though, you're on your own. You hurt me, Jess, in just about every way possible. I'm working on forgiving you, but you don't get to be part of my life again."

Silence stretched across the line. Had the call dropped? "Okay. I'll make the arrangements and send you an email with the details. Thanks, Colin."

"Yeah." He pushed end and drummed his fingers on his leg. He had some details to arrange himself.

Colin was one of the first passengers off the ferry. That was certainly one bonus of traveling light. The bulkiest item he had was his guitar, but even it was easy enough to sling over his shoulder. The rest of his instruments were packed carefully among his clothes in his hiking backpack. It was a risk to trade out the hard fiddle case for a soft one, but since he'd be toting his own things, he'd remember to be careful. The flexibility was worth the hassle. He followed the signs to the bus terminal and booked a ride into Paris. Four more hours of sitting. At least on the ferry he'd been able to walk around. And as soon as he hit Paris, he'd be trading the bus seat for an airplane seat. Hopefully Jessica sprang for first class. If she hadn't...he'd pay for the upgrade himself. Even if meant he had to wait for a different flight. He had a hotel reservation at the Marriott on Pennsylvania Avenue, and that's where he'd meet with the board of his old company. Jessica had reassured him that she'd still be in Chicago. So at least he didn't have to worry about that. To be safe, he'd given himself two extra days in D.C. You never knew what kind of delays you were going to face when dealing with the airlines. He didn't care about the board having to reschedule, but there was too much at stake in Annapolis to risk the timing.

He turned to stare out the window. The French countryside zipped past. He'd come back and explore another time—it was beautiful. Maybe he'd learn a word or two of French first. Maybe Rachel spoke French.

His trek from the bus station to the airport, through security and onto the plane was a blur. He would've booked a cabin on the ferry and gotten a few hours of good sleep if he'd known this much more travel waited for him on the other end. Settled into his first class seat, he pulled the shade and closed his eyes. With luck, he could get in a good nap.

Before he knew it, the captain was on the intercom asking them to prepare for landing. How he'd managed to sleep without waking for the duration of the flight was a mystery, but he was grateful for the rest. He almost felt refreshed. Almost. Colin pushed open the window shade and watched as they followed the Potomac River past Arlington Cemetery and the Pentagon into the airport. It was one of the prettiest landings he could remember, though bumpy.

His eyes ached from too little sleep. Catnaps here and there were fine for a time, but he needed a serious rest. Prone. With customs behind him, Colin gathered his bags and got into the taxi line.

19

Rachel slipped onto a stool at the kitchen island and poured a cup of tea from the freshly brewed pot. Her time in Ireland had convinced her that an afternoon tea break was a necessity. Some of the best conversations she'd had with Colin had been over a pot of tea. Colin...her heart grew heavy...she hadn't heard from him in more than a week. Had he made it to France? She'd expected an email, maybe a call. She missed his voice.

She swallowed the burning lump in her throat and blinked back tears. She wasn't going to cry over him anymore. Too many tears had already soaked her pillow on his account. She was an entrepreneur, a successful one. Or, at least, she would be. Reservations were picking up. She had a honeymooning couple checking in tonight, along with the older couple already checked-in, and a single reserved for the weekend, with the possibility of an extension for the week.

The phone rang. She smiled. Maybe this was another reservation.

"Good afternoon, Snowy Egret Inn, may I help you?"

"Is that you then, Rachel? It's Siobhan."

Her smile widened into a grin and spread across her face. "Oh, Aunt Siobhan, it's so lovely to hear from you. How are you and Patrick doing?"

"We're grand, though we miss you, m'dear. After being on my own for so long, I never expected to want so many people around, but now…I'm thinking of closing down for a bit in the winter and coming out to see you."

"I'd love to have you, of course, but can Patrick close down the pub?"

"Oh, no. But his staff could run things for a week or so if he took the time off. And, truth be told, he's thinking of hiring a full-time manager, says now he's married to me he doesn't want to be married to the pub as well."

Rachel laughed. "You do both have businesses that run your lives. How's the Sea Haven?"

"Jam packed. The tourists are out in full swing. I'm loving every minute of it. We had the most charming couple from France last week."

Her aunt rambled about the guests and their travel plans. Rachel smiled. The happiness in her aunt's voice wasn't solely due to the B&B's guests. Patrick hollered from the background periodically to correct or add to her aunt's retelling. They sounded as if they'd been married for years.

"Have you heard from Colin? The pub's not the same without his music in the evenings."

She sipped her tea. "I've had an email or two. I think he was off to France, in fact, but I've not heard if he made it there."

Which wasn't her business. After all, it wasn't as if they were even dating. Sure, they'd been moving in that direction if those scintillating kisses were any indication. But…she obviously hadn't been enough to tempt him to settle down. No matter that her lips still tingled when she thought of him.

"Oh, well. That's disappointing. I was so sure that the two of you…"

"I know, Aunt Siobhan. But it's fine. It's good. I have the inn now, so it's not as if I have a ton of time for extracurricular entanglements. You know how that is."

"I do, dear. I know exactly." A hint of sadness tinged her aunt's voice. Siobhan cleared her throat. "Tell me about your customers. You sent me the photos, so I've got a grand mental picture of your place formed, but what sort of people are you seeing?"

Rachel rubbed her chest and pushed away the lingering image of Colin. She told her aunt about George and Silvia, as well as the Navy parents she'd hosted and the upcoming honeymooners. Her aunt was pleased that she'd replaced the more American breakfast menu with options for a full Irish or lighter continental fare. Rachel didn't bother mentioning that she left off the puddings. She had no idea where she'd even find them in Annapolis, and didn't care enough to search them out. There was only so far she'd go in the name of authenticity.

"And the town, are you settling in? Feeling at home?"

"I am. It's not Kinsale…but where is?"

Her aunt laughed. "Nowhere but here. You sound happy and well. I'm proud of you. Your da would be, too, I think."

"I hope so." Rachel finished her tea and glanced at the clock above the stove. "I ought to run and be sure the rooms are ready for my guests tonight. They could be here any time now. Thanks so much for calling."

"Talk again soon, Rachel dear. And figure out when in the winter you want us. We'll be there."

The guests were tucked in for the night. Rachel sat on the overstuffed chintz sofa that George and Silvia had left in their living room. It wasn't her taste, but it was comfortable. For now, that was all that mattered. She propped her feet on the small walnut coffee table and opened her laptop.

Her aunt's phone call had been delightful, but it had dug up all the longing for Colin she'd thought she'd buried. She opened her personal email. Nothing. She'd tried to reconnect with old friends from the Shenandoah, but Annapolis might as well be a world away with the busy families people her age were building. It didn't matter. It couldn't. She was, slowly, making friends with her neighbors, plugging in at her church. It would take time for them to be fully entrenched, but the tiniest tendrils of roots were digging in to her new home.

She logged into her domain provider and made a few tweaks to the inn's website. Several new comments from the guestbook in the foyer were worthy of the testimonials page. She clicked through the various travel websites to check for reviews. There were two new comments—both, thankfully, positive. She sent the guests a quick email thanking them for taking the time to leave a rating and reminding them to sign up for her newsletter announcing special offers. Finally, she logged into her favorite social media site.

Rachel skimmed through her news feed, and then clicked on Colin's name from her friend list. No new updates. Why hadn't he mentioned something about the ferry ride to France? Or Paris? Was he even going to go to Paris? Didn't you have to, if you went to France? Sighing, she flipped to her email and started a new message.

Hey Colin, I hope you're doing well in France. Is the cheese as wonderful as everyone says? Paris is on my bucket list, though I don't think I'll be dipping into that bucket anytime soon. The inn is keeping me on my toes – two new guests tonight, another for the weekend (possibly longer – fingers crossed!)

Anyway...I miss you.

-Rachel

Her fingers hovered over the delete key. Was it too much to say she missed him? What if he didn't miss her? But...what if he did? She'd pricked his pride enough to recognize that he wasn't likely to be the first to bring it up. Men. Rachel frowned. Maybe she should—no. Before she could change her mind she clicked send and let out a breath.

20

Colin checked his watch. The suits were going to be late if they didn't hurry up. He wasn't going to wait much beyond their appointment time, either. There were museums to discover, monuments to conquer.

"Mr. O'Bryan?" A front desk staff member paused by his chair.

"Yes?"

"There's a group of gentlemen here to see you. They've reserved the conference room. It's on B-one, near the business center."

"Thanks." Colin shook his head. That wasn't the agreement. But he could play their game. He might be a bit rusty, but he had no doubt his sharp business skills would come back in short order. He descended the stairs and paused to admire the waterfall that flowed down the wall by the elevator. Tucking his hands in the pockets of his khakis, he strolled down the hallway toward the meeting.

Everyone was seated when he pushed open the door. They'd arranged themselves at the head of the table, the position of power. Strong arm tactics must be the name of the game. He offered a smile and a brief nod. "Gentlemen."

"Colin. It's so nice to meet you in person. We've heard such good things." The man at the head of the table spoke without standing. "Have a seat."

Colin pulled out a chair next to one of the flunkies on the left side of the table causing eyebrows to lift. They'd expected him to sit at the other end. Well, he wasn't playing the game their way.

The man at the head of the table cleared his throat. "Okay. Great. Um. I'm Charles Cooper, President of the Board. To my left is..."

"Chuck. Can I call you Chuck?" Colin smirked. "Let's cut to the chase and save all of us some time. You want me to head up a government arm of my old company. Jessica probably told you that wasn't going to happen. She probably told you that multiple times. But apparently you didn't listen or you don't want to hear it. So let me reiterate it for you, in person, so there's no doubt. I'm not interested. I'm only meeting with you to get you off Jessica's back about it. And if she has any sense at all, she's already taking steps to make sure this situation can't happen again."

"I see." Charles narrowed his eyes and stared at Colin for a moment before picking up the glass of water in front of him and taking a long drink. They hadn't offered Colin anything, though he suspected that was supposed to have come after all the buddy-buddy introductions. He hadn't missed this aspect of the corporate world at all…and it was the primary reason he'd been adamant that his company—back when it had been his company—wasn't going to take investor money. "You're not interested in hearing the details of our offer?"

"I'm really not. Returning to the corporate world isn't currently something on my radar."

Charles looked down at the folder in front of him. "You're having success as a traveling musician then, I take it?"

The condescension in Charles' voice made Colin bristle. He shouldn't be surprised that they knew what he'd been doing, but it irked him just the same. He sucked in air and pasted on a fake smile. *Stay calm.*

"Actually, yes. Though that's also not a long term proposition." Colin pushed his chair back and stood. "But really, if I decide to sell peanuts on the street corner in New York City, it's none of your concern. I cashed out according to the terms set forth by your board and have been adhering to the restrictions of the non-compete agreement you demanded. Beyond that, I'm not sure what else there is to say other than good luck with your government contracts, gentlemen."

Colin strode from the room, his blood pounding in his ears. That could've gone better. But what gave them the right to look down on his choices? Had everyone thought he'd just fall in line with Jessica's ploys? His cell phone rang.

"Yes?"

"You didn't even hear them out? What is this, Colin? You said you'd talk to them." Jessica's panic oozed through the phone.

"I did talk to them, I told them what I told you. I'm not interested. That ought to get them off your back. And, like I told them, I hope you're putting things in place to keep them from railroading you again. 'Cause next time you're just going to lose the company, and that'd be a shame. We worked hard to build it, Jess. Don't mess it up." Colin pushed end. Almost immediately it rang again. He sent the call to voicemail and powered down his phone. Next stop, the Washington Monument. Maybe an elevated view would restore his perspective.

Saturday afternoon, Colin parked his rental car along the curb outside the Snowy Egret Inn. He looked over the brick building and its gleaming white porches and smiled. Did she realize how well it suited her? He took a deep breath to calm the jitters that threatened to take over and grabbed his overnight bag from the back seat. He could get the rest of his luggage later.

He pressed the buzzer by the front door and waited. Was he supposed to just walk in? She was expecting him—well, a guest at least. He'd fudged his name a little, not wanting to spoil the surprise. Footsteps approached and locks clicked before the door swung open.

"Welcome to the…" Rachel's welcoming smile faltered. "Colin."

He waited as her mouth opened and shut.

"You said check-in was at three." He set down his bag and moved a step closer. "You also said you missed me."

Rachel nodded.

Colin closed the distance between them and slid his hand around her neck, twining his fingers through her hair. "I missed you, too. I tried not to…it didn't work so well."

He lowered his lips to hers. She sank into him, her arms wrapping around his shoulders. Colin sent up a brief prayer of thanksgiving.

Rachel stepped back, a smile tugging at the corner of her mouth. "And now you've experienced the traditional Snowy Egret welcome. Come on in, and I'll show you to your room."

Colin couldn't stop the burst of laughter. "If that's the traditional welcome, I'll be sure to visit often."

"I put you in one of the back rooms overlooking the patio. But if you want balcony access, I can switch you." Rachel led the way up the main stairs.

"A back room is fine. Rachel…"

She stopped and pushed open the door to his room, offering him the key. "The smaller gold key is for the front door so you can come and go as you like. The larger, old-timey key is to your room. I'll let you get settled."

"Rach…."

She stopped at the top of the back set of stairs and turned.

He closed his eyes. Had he misread things after all? "Will you go for a walk with me this evening?"

Rachel gazed at him for several ticks of the grandfather clock in the downstairs hallway. His heart thundered.

"You can take me to dinner. Five o'clock."

He watched her disappear down the stairs. Two hours.

As the clock chimed five, Colin stood in the foyer fighting the urge to pace. Though the place he had in mind was casual, he'd changed into black slacks and a cobalt dress shirt. It was as close to formal as he could get with the limited wardrobe he'd brought. Rachel came down the hallway from the back of the first floor, a skirt in a riot of colors floating around her ankles.

"You look amazing."

She smiled. "I could say the same. I was thinking we could…"

"I got it. I did a little research and found the perfect place." Colin offered his elbow.

Rachel hesitated before she slipped her arm through his. "All right, lead on."

"It's just a few blocks, but we can drive if you want?"

She shook her head. "It's a nice night for walking, not too hot, not too muggy. You don't get a ton of evenings like this in the summer, even with the breeze off the water."

He set a slow pace, enjoying the companionship and light conversation. Every time he tried to bring up Ireland, she deftly changed the subject. Would she give him the chance to explain, or had he missed that opportunity?

Before long, he stopped in front of a restaurant that overlooked the water. "How about here? I've heard good things. Well, read them online at least."

Rachel looked up at the sign for O'Flaherty's. Her cheeks took on a rosy glow. "I haven't actually been in here yet. I keep meaning to but…"

"But?"

She frowned and turned to face him. "Everything Irish reminds me of you. I know I'm the one who left, but you weren't going to stay. And I…I needed a home."

"Have you found one?"Colin squeezed her fingers gently.

"I don't know yet." Rachel looked out over the water. "The inn should be enough. Maybe in time it will be."

A tiny flicker of hope sparked in his heart. "Maybe you need to realize what I've recently come to understand. Home and roots and stability? They don't come from a place or a building. They come from the people you love and those who love you in return. Traveling around Ireland, I never got homesick until I met you…and then left without you. It's why I came back to Kinsale.

And then you went away and you took my heart with you." Colin placed his fingers gently on her chin and turned her toward him. "So I came to find you, because I love you."

Rachel's lower lip trembled as her eyes searched his face. A tear escaped, trailing down her cheek. He tenderly brushed it away with his thumb. She tilted her head and swallowed hard. He leaned in, pulled her close, and wrapped his arms around her.

"Welcome home," she whispered. "Welcome home."

Author's Note

Thank you for reading *Kinsale Kisses.* I hope that you enjoyed the time spent within these pages. If you did, I would appreciate it if you'd help others enjoy it too by leaving a review on Amazon and Goodreads and telling your friends about it. Any success my books have is owed to readers like you who take the time to tell others about my stories. Thank you, from the bottom of my heart.

Ireland has long held a place in my heart. Even before my husband and I first visited in 2003, I dreamed of Ireland. Being there in person didn't disappoint. I'm grateful to have had two opportunities to visit the amazing country and to interact with the friendly and delightful people who live there. The places Rachel and Colin visit are all real, save for The Flat Tire and The Sea Haven B&B (though friendly pubs and B&Bs are easy to find all through Ireland and you'll never be disappointed by a decision to visit them.) Any inaccuracies in the descriptions are my own.

Thanks, as always, go out to my critique partner and beta readers, without whom I'd be lost. And, most importantly, to my Heavenly Father who continues to give me stories and the desire to write them down.

About the Author

Elizabeth Maddrey began writing stories as soon as she could form the letters properly and has never looked back. Though her practical nature and love of math and organization steered her into computer science for college and graduate school, she has always had one or more stories in progress to occupy her free time. When she isn't writing, Elizabeth is a voracious consumer of books and has mastered the art of reading while undertaking just about any other activity. Elizabeth is a member of ACFW and lives in the suburbs of Washington D.C. with her husband and their two incredibly active little boys.

Visit her website at www.ElizabethMaddrey.com

www.Facebook.com/ElizabethMaddrey

www.twitter.com/elizabethmaddre